"I'_____
Terri replied as she efficiently wrapped a towel
around his waist and tucked it in securely. She
took his arm to help him step into the shower,
then stepped in after him. "Now, sit on the
stool."

"This is no fun."

Terri moved around behind him and adjusted
the water temperature. As she faced his bare
back with the hand-held shower attachment,
she wondered if she should make the water
temperature a lot colder. "Do you want fun? Or
do you want a shower?"

"I want a shower, but I—"

A blast of warm water on the back of his neck
stopped his words. He sighed and let his head
fall forward. Terri almost sighed, too. She was
suffering from a variety of sensations: caution,
longing, arousal....

"Can I get rid of this towel now?" Michael asked.
"It's not really hiding anything."

Terri's eyes lowered to his lap. He was right.
The wet weight of the thick cloth left *nothing* to
the imagination.

"I may be injured, but I'm not dead."

SUPER ROMANCE

Author **Lyn Ellis** has made quite an entrance into the publishing world. Her first book, *Dear John...*, was not only a RITA finalist in two categories, but it also won the Waldenbooks award for the bestselling Harlequin of 1994. Not bad for a first novel! This talented writer lives in Atlanta, Georgia, where she spends her time coming up with wonderful story ideas to delight her newfound, dedicated audience.

Books by Lyn Ellis

HARLEQUIN TEMPTATION
488—DEAR JOHN...
532—IN PRAISE OF YOUNGER MEN

Don't miss any of our special offers. Write to us at the following address for information on our newest releases.

Harlequin Reader Service
U.S.: 3010 Walden Ave., P.O. Box 1325, Buffalo, NY 14269
Canadian: P.O. Box 609, Fort Erie, Ont. L2A 5X3

MICHAEL'S ANGEL
Lyn Ellis

Harlequin Books

TORONTO • NEW YORK • LONDON
AMSTERDAM • PARIS • SYDNEY • HAMBURG
STOCKHOLM • ATHENS • TOKYO • MILAN
MADRID • WARSAW • BUDAPEST • AUCKLAND

Thanks to:
Donna Sterling for making me pitch this book. And, as always, Anne, Ann, Sandra and Pat. My brother-in-law, Jim, the intrepid sailor who swears he only runs aground when I'm in the boat. Pam and Bob Barker for the use of their treehouse—where I first met Michael's Angel.
My medical advisors: Fay Kilgore, MN, CMM/Author
Ellen Taber, Surgical nurse/Author
Bitsy Bird, MN, Nursing supervisor and the 'other' mother
DJ Feather, Pediatric Respiratory Therapist
And to Andria Bramlett for letting me share her family.
Finally, to Brenda, for nudging me past my comfort zone.

ISBN 0-373-25675-2

MICHAEL'S ANGEL

Copyright © 1996 by Gin Ellis.

Prologue

MICHAEL WELDON wished he was dead. As dead as his marriage, as dead as his son, Josh.

He aimed the bow of his sailboat, *Destiny*, into the wind and studied the distant Florida coastline. It was a perfect day. Bright but not sultry, with a few fluffy cumulus clouds in the sky. Seas were two to three feet, winds ten to fifteen knots from the southeast. To be free and tacking into the wind on a day like this should be everything a man could wish for. Any man except him.

Michael wished he was dead.

The boat bucked slightly and the sail snapped as the wind shifted. Michael's hand automatically adjusted the tiller. He wasn't looking at the rise of the waves or the cut of the bow. He was staring into the past, reliving the tragic events of that day two years ago that had effectively ended his life, ended everything he'd loved and counted on. The fact that he'd physically survived that day didn't mean a damned thing. He was a dead man walking around with a beating heart.

Each time he saw the ocean, the memories came back. Stupid. Stupid. Stupid. *Why had he been so stupid?* Why hadn't he said no?

Because Josh had been so excited.

The three of them, Josh, his wife, Terri, and Michael had taken a long three-day sail to the Florida Keys. One of the marinas they stopped at had wave runners for rent. As other, older boys sped by, Josh had watched mesmerized, willing to trade the next five years of his allowance for a ride.

Please, Dad.

Why hadn't Michael said no? He felt as though his lungs might explode from the guilt and pain. He didn't say no because Josh's hero, Super-Dad, seldom said no. What harm could it do to rent a wave runner for an hour or two to take his son for a ride? he'd explained to Terri when she'd questioned the idea.

They'd gotten dumped twice. Once from hitting the wake of another boat and once when he'd let Josh steer and the boy had turned too sharply. They'd floundered around in the water laughing and struggling to get back on the wave runner. It was all just part of the fun. Josh could swim and he was also wearing a life jacket. So why, when they were dumped into the water the third time, had Josh gone under? Why, when Michael managed to reach him, was he as limp as a bundle of rags? Michael blinked to clear the salt spray out of his eyes. The pain of that moment—the moment he'd dragged his son's still body from the water—remained as sharp as a razor. Cutting deeper each time he relived it. Michael knew Josh's death was his fault. He'd give anything to have died that day instead of his son.

Then he wouldn't have had to face Terri. He wouldn't have had to stand by helplessly and watch her methodically and rationally use every trick of her pediatric nurse's training to try to bring their son back to life. But her training hadn't worked, her silent tears and his fervent prayers hadn't worked. When the paramedics arrived, he'd had to drag Terri away from Josh. She'd screamed and fought him. It was one of the last times Michael had touched her, really touched her. It was the last time he'd been able to look her in the eye.

Everything had died that day. Their future, their family, their marriage. All the love Michael had ever needed or wanted. And now he was faced with the reality of divorce, of having to return to West Palm Beach to appear before a judge and sign the papers to formally end his marriage. The formality didn't matter. Nothing mattered.

Lost in memories, he couldn't tell how much time had passed, but he noticed a few gray clouds had gathered on the horizon forming a squall line to the southeast. And the wind seemed to be picking up steadily. Maybe the day wouldn't turn out so perfect, after all.

Michael smiled at the prospect and tacked the boat directly toward the coming storm.

Michael wished he was dead.

1

TERRI WELDON had just stirred a spoonful of sugar into her cup of coffee when she heard the page. Damn! It never failed. Take a break and the emergency room goes on alert. She managed to swallow one mouthful of coffee on the way to the trash receptacle. After being on duty for nearly twelve hours, working her own shift and part of someone else's, she'd need something besides adrenaline to keep her going. The strain of the last three days had taken its toll.

Her friend Anna, who also worked in the ER, met Terri at the swinging doors of the unit. "We have a Coast Guard helicopter coming in." Anna reached over to grip Terri's arm. The look on her friend's face made Terri stop in her tracks. "It's Michael. They've found Michael."

"Are you sure?" Terri could barely utter the words. She'd been stunned when she'd read the headline that had run in the *Palm Beach Post* a few days before: Local Attorney, Michael Weldon, Missing After Sailboat, *Destiny,* Founders In Storm

At Sea. The room went fuzzy for a moment. They'd found Michael. He'd been missing for nearly three days and she'd thought . . . no, she had refused to think.

"They located his ID." Anna pulled Terri toward the group preparing a stretcher. "They should be here in fifteen minutes."

"He's alive, then?" Terri needed to hear the words, to know.

"He's alive but he's got irregular respiration. Possible broken ribs, collapsed lung and—" she hesitated slightly "—there's head trauma."

Terri's knees weakened. *Michael.*

"Maybe you should sit this one out," Anna said.

"No. I need to see him." Terri was already walking toward the door. "I need to know he's alive."

THEY WERE on the roof when the helicopter touched down; Dr. Hubbard, an intern, three nurses, one orderly and Terri. Backwash from the blades whipped around them as the helicopter door slid open. One Coast Guardsman dressed in a fluorescent-orange flight suit jumped to the ground and turned to pull a stretcher forward.

To Terri, the scene unfolded in slow motion. She froze, welded to the landing pad as she watched a man being shifted to the rolling stretcher. Not a man—Michael . . . her husband. She almost couldn't recognize him. He was burned from three days in the harsh Florida sun, his face swollen and puffy. He'd been intubated and three strips of white tape were plastered across the lower part of his face to hold the breathing tube in place. She'd never seen him so helpless.

She remained paralyzed. Terri heard the Coast Guard medic reciting the medical status of Michael's injuries, but it merely became a jumble of words. She stared at Michael's face, at the lax features of someone who was obviously deeply unconscious. She hadn't seen him or touched him in over a year, and now he'd been delivered to her more than half-dead.

"This guy must have a strong will to live," the medic yelled over the whine of the helicopter as he helped strap Michael onto the stretcher. "Even with a head injury and broken ribs, he managed to tie himself to a cooler cover. The divers said that the lines were so tight, they had to cut him loose."

A strong will to live. Terri fought back panic. For the last two years, she'd been consumed by grief for Josh, never considering the possibility that Michael could die, too. She pushed her way between the nurses as the orderly rolled the stretcher toward the rooftop elevator.

"Michael?" She leaned over and lightly touched his face with a trembling hand. *"Michael."* But he didn't respond.

ANNA STOPPED at the doors of the unit and pulled Terri away.

Terri pulled back. "I have to help him."

"No," Anna said and increased her grip.

Inside the ER, the medical team was already efficiently moving into their trauma routine. Terri watched as one of the nurses used surgical scissors to cut away what was left of Michael's clothes. The respiratory therapist had already begun to bag him, forcing him to breathe.

Dr. Hubbard, who Terri knew well, spared one sympathetic glance at her, then ordered a nurse to pull the curtain shut.

"You can't help him," Anna said and tugged Terri toward the nurses' room in the back of the ER. "You'd only be in the way. Let them get him stabilized."

Meekly, Terri followed Anna, not because she wanted to, but because she knew Anna was right. At the moment, she was so shocked she could barely remember her own name. How would she ever be able to help Michael?

"TERRI?"

"Yes?" she answered and stood to face the doctor. She'd seen John Hubbard give bad news or hope to hundreds of other family members. As she faced him for her own news, a freshly sharpened edge of pain cut into her heart. She'd wanted to end her marriage to Michael, to go on with her life. But not like this. Not like Josh.

"He's stabilized, with spontaneous respiration and heartbeat but he's in very serious condition. Now, the head injury is our main concern. We haven't been able to get him to respond to stimulus. I've sent him downstairs for a CAT scan. Other than that, he's got a separated shoulder and a few broken ribs. There's an air leak in the left lung so we put in a chest tube. He's dehydrated and suffering from exposure. But, he's alive, and very lucky."

Terri let out the breath she'd been holding. "More stubborn than lucky." She managed a slight smile for Dr. Hubbard, but the pain in her chest remained. Michael had always been healthy and vital and now he was so hurt. "When can I see him?"

MICHAEL COULDN'T SEE. He couldn't tell if his eyes were open or shut. The light was so bright that, for a moment, he thought the angel had come back. The angel. A sense of urgency pushed through his confusion. He squinted to make out the shapes and forms around him. That's when he saw Terri sitting in a chair not two feet from his bed. His *wife*, sitting with her eyes shut and her head angled back, resting, as though she'd been waiting a long time.

He could almost touch her. The midnight black hair that spilled across one shoulder, the high, sexy slant of the cheekbones she'd inherited from her French ancestors. He knew how her hair smelled, the soft texture of her skin, how her blue eyes used to widen and grow dark when she looked at him. The way she used to sigh his name when they made love. His Theresa Anne Mitchell—his Tam, utterly familiar, and yet, for the first time, he felt as though he could really see her. His whole body relaxed. He was alive. He had one more chance.

He tried to form her name, but his lips were stiff and swollen. He swallowed, the pain and the salty taste of his own blood reminding him of the storm, of the ocean. Of the angel.

Terri . . . Tam.

As if she'd heard him, her eyes fluttered open. She didn't move. She just stared at him for a moment, disbelieving. Suddenly, she blinked and straightened in the chair, then leaned closer to touch his hand.

"Michael?" Her fingers were cool and smooth. His arm twitched with the desire to grip her hand tightly. To never let her go.

She withdrew as if she'd hurt him. "You're going to be all right." Her voice was as soothing as the stroke of her hand had been, and as welcome. God, he'd missed her.

Michael wanted to speak, to tell her how glad he was to see her. To tell her the amazing things that had happened to him. But trying to form the words made his head pound. Tears of frustration blurred his vision. Terri's face swam before his eyes and he felt her touch on his arm once more. He didn't want her to go. *Tam*.

"Dr. Hubbard says you're going to be all right," she said again, as if he wouldn't take her word for it. Then her face drifted away, receded. He felt as though he was sinking through a tunnel into the darkness . . .

THE STORM HAD COME out of the southeast like a five-thousand-foot wall moving with the speed of a hell-bound locomotive. The sight of it had momentarily snatched the breath from Michael's heaving lungs, while the change of air pressure had pounded in his ears like an enormous heartbeat. As he'd paused in his single-handed struggle to keep the *Destiny* into the wind, the ocean came alive, churning, rising beneath the boat to greet the rolling clouds and the angry air. In that moment, Michael knew he'd truly tempted fate this time. He'd always held the slim hope that someday he'd get over Josh's death, that someday Terri would look at him with love in her eyes again.

He wasn't sure when it registered that "someday" had slipped away from him. Was it the first time he realized that the swells were so huge and the rain so furious he couldn't see the horizon anymore? Or was it when the largest breaker he'd ever seen rolled the *Destiny* on her side and tossed him, struggling with lines and debris, into deep, cold water? Alone.

Then darkness. A piece of boat, or water, or sky had hit him over the head. Some detached voice inside Michael had shrugged and said, "This is it."

This is it? the fearful, very human part of him echoed in alarm; the part of him that intended to live forever no matter how bad living hurt. Then there was a sharp tug and a snapping sound. In the space of a blink, he was suspended in the air, above a man—above a body—that floated facedown in the deep blue ocean water.

Poor guy, he thought. *He's a goner.* A wave rocked the man sideways and tightened the coil of line caught around one muscular arm. An arm graced by a solid-gold watch, a hand adorned with a wedding ring. Michael looked a little closer. He recognized the expensive, sky blue polo shirt being pummeled by the heavy rain. *I used to have a shirt just like . . .* Realization punched the detachment out of him. He was looking at himself. At his own body.

And that would mean, he must be . . . dead?

A pulse of panic preceded an explosion of brilliant shimmering light. So bright he was overwhelmed, forced to close his eyes, and even then the radiance beat through his eyelids like a nuclear sun. Instantly, the storm and the water and the wind—everything—stopped. His ears rang with the lack of sound. In what could have been a millisecond, or an eternity later, Michael had slowly opened his eyes and looked into the face of an angel.

TERRI LEANED closer to Michael's ravaged face. He'd been unconscious for hours, but now he seemed to be stirring. "What did you say?" she asked, staunchly resisting the urge to smooth her fingers over his sunburned forehead. She knew from experience that Michael didn't need or want her touch. His eyes were nearly swollen shut but his mouth twitched again, trying to force out a word.

She listened intently. It sounded like "angel." A tug of disappointment tightened Terri's lips. He had to be delirious. He'd never called *her* angel.

He'd called her Tam.

"Anyone can call you Terri," he'd said, what seemed like a million years ago, when they'd been so happy, so in love. Before Josh.

Before Michael had abandoned her.

Tears flooded Terri's eyes, and for a moment she let down the guard she'd so carefully maintained for months. She'd realized she had to end her marriage to Michael, and three months ago she'd started the process, even though her heart wanted to cling to the one tiny part of all the happiness she'd ever known. Their marriage had given her Josh.

Oh, Michael. Terri lowered her head and rested her cheek against his uninjured arm. So many times in the past, she had needed his touch, needed to share her pain with the only other person in the world who might understand. But he hadn't been there. Grief rose inside her like a wave, threatening to drown her with her own tears. Would she ever stop crying for Josh, stop wishing that she'd been able to change what happened? She'd given up her job as a private pediatric nurse, committed her life and most of her time to working in the ER.

How many people would she have to save until she had paid for not saving her son?

"Tam?" It was barely a whisper, but it brought her back from the past with a jolt. She quickly raised her head and swiped the tears on her cheeks.

Terri ripped open one of the lemon-scented moisturizing wipes from a pile on the bedside table and carefully swabbed Michael's dry lips so they wouldn't crack when he moved them. His eyes flickered open a fraction wider at her touch. Was he trying to smile? Early in their marriage, she'd discovered that she was a sucker for his boyish, pirate grin. But he'd lost that smile after Josh.

"Do you want some water?" At his slight nod, she busied herself with the cup and the bendable straw. After he'd taken a few swallows, she fished a small piece of ice out of the cup and slipped it into his mouth.

"Does your head hurt?"

He merely sucked on the ice and stared at her.

"Michael? Does your head—"

He swallowed, briefly closed his eyes and frowned. When he looked at her again, he appeared to be in pain.

"No," he said, forcing out the word. He seemed to be struggling against the pull of unconsciousness.

Worried, Terri tried to help him focus. "No, your head doesn't hurt?"

"No," he said again, jaw clenched with the struggle of forming the next word. Terri leaned closer again, concerned over the effort he seemed to be making to communicate. What was so important?

He grimaced, and one of his hands moved. Terri thought she'd lost him to oblivion once more, but he stirred and ran his tongue over his lower lip.

"No...divorce."

"What?" Terri managed to say. His whispered words had blared at her like an air horn, but she couldn't believe her ears. "What did you say?"

No answer. Michael appeared to have expended his reservoir of energy. He slipped into unconsciousness, leaving Terri to struggle with reality alone. It was all she could do not to shake him. What did any of this have to do with their divorce? A hollow feeling blossomed in her stomach. Did Michael even know what he was saying? Had he forgotten the reason he'd come back to West Palm in the first place? To sign the divorce agreement?

"Has he come around yet?"

Lost in her own thoughts, Terri jumped at the sound of Anna's voice. She pushed away from Michael's bedside. "He was awake a few moments ago. I gave him some water."

Anna moved over to get a good look at Terri. She didn't seem to like what she saw. "If you don't go home and get some rest, we'll have to assign you a bed." Anna rested her hand on Michael's forearm above the IV needle, and then against the pulse in his neck. "You know he's better off unconscious for a while. With those broken ribs, merely breathing is going to hurt like the devil. Did he recognize you?"

"Yes, I think so. But he said something odd."

"Odd?"

Terri could feel color rising in her cheeks. "I mean, it has nothing to do with—" She cleared her throat. "He mentioned something about our divorce."

Anna stared at her for a few seconds. "Well, don't worry. All in all, he's actually in pretty good shape. If he's a little delirious, that's to be expected." Anna squeezed Terri's arm. "You go home for a few hours. I know you're worried about him slipping into a coma. I'll keep an eye on him and call you if anything changes."

Terri turned and searched the eerily expressionless features of the only man she had ever loved. Michael's breathing seemed shallow but regular. It was so difficult to control her urge to touch him, to soothe him, even now. When he'd left her, loving him had been a hard habit to break. Having him appear in her life again, hurt and helpless, brought back echoes of that love with a vengeance. But Terri knew Michael didn't want her touch or her concern. He had walked away from that a long time ago.

Anna made one final argument. "You heard what the Coast Guard guy said. Michael is a fighter."

"I don't know about that," Terri answered. "But he can be incredibly stubborn." As the reverberation of her own voice hung in the air, Terri remembered the first words Michael had spoken after being brought back from death's door. *No divorce.*

THE ANGEL LOOKED like Sean Connery, with an attitude. Even the fact that light seemed to spill through his image didn't lessen the effect of those eyes, those worldly-wise, yet otherworldly, features. This angel was a warrior, ready to fight for Michael's life, and his soul.

The power of the angel's presence held Michael in awe, but he wasn't afraid, not like the first time—when he'd been dead. Michael briefly wondered if he was awake or dreaming now, as if it mattered. His entire world looked different.

He knew he was alive.

And, he knew he and Terri couldn't have prevented Josh's death. That "knowing" was a relief beyond description, beyond forgiveness, and he wanted to share that comfort with Terri. He hadn't figured out why he'd been given another chance after getting himself killed, but the angel had sent him back.

Now the angel stood over him with a presence larger than mere life. Grace and love and forgiveness incarnate, delivered with the bright, singing sharpness of a sword.

You must remember. You have to save Terri. You are the only one who can.

"I've seen her," Michael said without making a sound.

Instead of a response, the angel brought one of his bright hands to rest on Michael's chest, directly over his heart. The rigid tightness in his lungs instantly eased, and Michael felt the very blood in his veins answer the call of life in that touch.

You must remember.

"I've told her . . ." Michael's thoughts and his urgency floated away as the order to rest flowed through his skin. "I'll tell her . . . I remember."

2

WHOEVER INVENTED panty hose ought to be shot, Terri decided. Waves of heat swirled around her as she trudged across the blacktop parking lot toward the hospital. She'd always considered looking professional as part of her job. Although, each time she had to face the muggy Florida heat—in panty hose—she fantasized about spending her life in a pair of shorts.

It wasn't just the heat that had her nerves ruffled, though. It was Michael. Terri had arrived two hours early for her shift. She'd spent more time at the hospital in the past two days than anywhere else. Off duty or on, she'd made sure that Michael had everything he needed.

The question now was, why? The only acceptable answer was, for Josh. It couldn't be for Michael. Michael had abandoned her when she'd needed him most. When she'd needed to hold her husband because she'd never be able to hold her son again. She'd seen many patients close to death and her professional half had always risen to the occasion to do everything possible to save them. But it had nearly killed her to see Michael suffering. And she'd stood there terrified and frozen. Why? She'd worked out her grief and her anger in counseling. And her love . . . she'd put that away. She and Michael had been living separate lives for over a year, or, the truth be told, since Josh's death, and now the time had come to get divorced and to go on.

So, why did the hungry look in Michael's eyes each time she walked into his room make her want to cry?

The welcome rush of cool air surrounded her as she entered the hospital through the automatic doors. She ran one hand along her collar to fluff the damp hair at her neck and adjusted her purse strap on her shoulder. She straightened her spine and walked toward the elevator. Caring for Michael was natural enough, her reason answered. He'd been her husband for nine years. He'd been her lover, her future . . . the father of her child. Terri punched the button for the fourth floor. She had begun planning a new future with the help of her counselor, one that might include working with children again as soon she felt ready. A future that had nothing to do with Michael Weldon.

MICHAEL WAS SITTING UP in bed when she arrived. Sitting up and surrounded by women. Two of the older, over-sixty, hospital volunteers, along with one who couldn't be more than eighteen, were tittering around Michael, as if he were Mel Gibson.

It should have made Terri smile, but for some reason it irritated her. Two days ago, Michael had been unconscious and she'd been scared out of her mind. Now he was sitting up, smiling and flirting with the hospital staff.

"Do I need an invitation for this party?" Terri asked as she moved into the room and immediately wished she could recall the words. She'd meant for her question to sound funny, but it had come out sounding like an admonition from a disapproving nun. The volunteers did a lot of good work at the hospital and she certainly didn't want to discourage them. Besides, she was living proof that Michael's charm was a force to be reckoned with. She'd married him because of it.

The volunteers stopped tittering.

Then Michael spoke up. "This is my wife, Terri," he said as if they were at an afternoon tea. As if he wasn't sitting in bed with nothing on but a rib splint and an injured-man version of his pirate grin.

"Oh, we know Terri," Mrs. Anderson said with a smile. "And I'm glad we ran into you. I wanted to thank you again for baking those cupcakes for our CF fund-raiser. The kids just loved the little faces you put on them. I wish you could have been there to see their reaction."

Terri had wanted to be there, had planned to help with the party as part of her new beginning, but at the last minute she'd chickened out. She hadn't felt ready to face a roomful of children. One step at a time, she reminded herself. She forced her face to relax. "I'm sorry, Mary, but you know how the ER is. It's hard to get away sometimes."

Mary looked at her for a few long seconds. "I know dear," she said. "But I hope you'll come next time."

"We really need to move along. We have two more floors to cover," the other volunteer, Mrs. Silverman, said as she gathered up the books and games and toiletries they carried to offer patients. The young volunteer just stood there looking at Michael. "Janine?" the older woman added.

Terri assumed the role of nurse rather than wife and busied herself checking Michael's medical chart. As the volunteers filed out of the room, Mary reached into the pocket of her smock where she kept surprises for children she encountered and dropped a piece of hard candy onto the chart in Terri's hand. "I know you like the watermelon flavor," she whispered and squeezed her arm. "See you later."

In a few minutes, the women were gone and she was alone with her husband. As she watched, all the spark seemed to fade out of him.

"I tell you what, I'm tired of lying in this bed," he said with a sigh. He touched the material on his chest. "Can you fix this thing?"

"Why didn't you ask one of the floor nurses to do this?" Terri muttered as she fumbled with the Velcro attached to the sagging rib splint wrapped around Michael's chest.

"I'd rather have you do it." Michael's voice sounded strained and he drew in a quick breath as she pulled the splint tighter. She tried to be gentle. She knew he had to be in pain, but he held himself perfectly still. After an extended beat of silence, he added, "It's been a long time since you touched me."

Terri froze and stared at her own hand resting on the smooth, familiar skin of Michael's muscular shoulder. It had been a very long time, nearly two years. Memories pulsed through her of touching and loving, of simply admiring her husband's broad shoulders and muscular back. And his chest . . . She remembered the warmth of his skin, the taste. Terri abruptly removed her hand, and then, with as little actual contact as possible, tucked in the edge of the Velcro to hold it secure. She was glad Michael was facing the opposite wall so that he couldn't see her expression. She wasn't sure if it would be angry or fearful. She didn't want to remember what she'd missed when he'd left her and how much she'd missed it. She moved around the bed to face him.

Before she could change the subject, Michael caught her left hand and traced the bones of her fingers with his thumb. Over the empty space where her wedding ring used to be.

"I like the way you touch me." He gazed up at her and drew in a slow breath. "For a while there, I thought you'd never touch me again."

Logical thought deserted Terri. She stared into the same intelligent, hazel eyes she'd known for years and saw a different man there. Someone she didn't recognize, but who mesmerized her just the same. The pull was so sweet, so strong, she stopped fighting for a moment and let it wash over her. She'd missed him so . . . and he'd come back. *No*, the logical part of her mind pointed out. *He came back to sign divorce papers, not to see you.* Silently cursing her overactive imagination, she yanked her hand away as if she'd been scorched. "Michael . . ." Her voice sounded strained, even to her own ears.

The door to the private room swung open, interrupting any words she might have added. Dr. Hubbard walked into the room followed by Marjorie, one of the day nurses.

"Here's our miracle patient," the doctor said as he lifted the chart from the slot at the end of the bed. "Sitting up, I see. I suppose you want to go home today."

Michael gave the doctor a pained smile. "Not today," he said. "As a matter of fact—" he grimaced "—I think I need to lie down."

He did look a little pale. When he moved, it was slowly, like a one-hundred-year-old man. After Terri helped him lie back, he took a few careful breaths and his color returned.

"Well, you're doing better than you have any right to be." The doctor pressed a stethoscope to Michael's chest. He listened for several moments then continued, "Having your own private nurse helps. You need to hurry and get well before Terri drives the nurses on this floor crazy." Dr. Hubbard smiled toward Terri and shoved the stethoscope back into his pocket. "Lung sounds are normal," he said to Marjorie. "How's your head?" he asked Michael. "Any pain? Dizziness?"

"I get dizzy if I move too fast, but the headaches are gone," Michael answered.

"Good—and you shouldn't be moving too fast. As I said, you're doing great. You just have to give your body some time to rest and recover."

After the doctor left, Terri glanced at her watch. She needed to get downstairs. "I've got to go. Is there anything else you need?"

"No." Michael looked tired, like a four-year-old fighting sleep . . . so much like his son. "I think I'll rest a while."

"Good." Terri swallowed against the unwanted memory of tucking Josh into bed and touched Michael's hand. The familiar habit of giving a quick good-night kiss caused her to lean over him. She caught herself halfway and pulled back. "I'll stop by later," she offered lamely and quit the room.

"WHAT'S HAPPENING to me?" she asked Tom Sizemore, her Employee Assistance counselor. After spending half her shift worrying about her reactions to Michael, she'd gone to see Tom on her break.

"You mean because you still care about your husband? You're a nurse, Terri. Nurses are notorious caretakers. He was part of your life, someone you had a personal interest in. Of course you are going to care about his well-being."

"But—"

"It's also perfectly natural for his accident to bring up old feelings. Have you talked with him about Josh?"

"No. And I don't want to." A rush of guilt and fear ran through Terri. She'd worked so hard to feel human again, to look at life as something other than torture, she couldn't—wouldn't—do anything that might bring back the pain. "I think I've finally come to grips with Josh's death and I don't want to go through the process again."

"It might be good for your husband. It might—"

"I'm sorry, but I don't know what to say to him—how to help him." She'd barely managed to help herself. "Besides, he never wanted to talk about it. He chose to disappear."

"You're still angry with him."

"Of course I'm angry." Terri felt like pounding on the desk. "I'm angry because a week ago I was finally feeling like I knew how to get on with my life. I had even talked myself into asking Dr. Perez about working in his office a couple days a week—working with children again. Two days later, Michael shows up, half-dead, scares a few years off my life, and now I'm so confused I don't know what to do."

"What do you want to do?"

Terri wanted to cry but she fought the urge. "I want to help Michael get well, and get him out of this hospital. I want to deal with reality, not think about what could have been."

"So he upsets you because he brings up the past?"

Terri lost her battle with the tears hovering in her eyes. They splashed down her cheeks. "He upsets me because he makes me wish for things I can never have."

The counselor passed a box of tissues to her. "What things?"

"A marriage. A family."

"Why do you think you can never have those things?"

The question surprised Terri. She'd been so caught up with Michael and the past, she'd forgotten that she still had a life ahead of her. She could remarry and possibly have another child. If she could find the courage.

But first she had to divorce Michael. To finish the process she'd begun three months ago. "I guess I meant I could never have those things again with Michael," she answered.

"Why?"

Why? her mind echoed. Because marriage and family meant love and support and she'd needed Michael, her husband, desperately, after Josh's death. When she couldn't cry, when she couldn't stop staring out windows so that she didn't have to see the sorrow on the faces around her. When her friends, whose children were alive and well, were afraid to talk to her. He was the only one who could have cried with her, who could have shared the pain and helped her bear it. But he'd been unable, or unwilling, to try.

Instead, on Mother's Day nearly a year after Josh's death, they'd fought. She'd been angry and crazy and finally able to cry. And Michael, furious or numb, relieved or afraid, couldn't handle it. He'd called Nancy, her sister. He'd bought Nancy a plane ticket, calmly waited for her to arrive. Then he'd sailed away the next morning, leaving everything—his job, his life, his wife, and her grief. That was WHY in capital letters. She could never trust him to be there for her in the future, not after that. Now she'd made new friends, had new plans and Michael wasn't included.

"Because I would keep on reliving Josh's death," *and my husband's abandonment.*

"Do you blame Michael for Josh's death?"

"No. I told you before, I never blamed Michael. I'm a nurse. *I* should have known about Josh's heart. I'm to blame, if anyone is."

"If you're realistic enough not to hold Michael responsible, then you also shouldn't paint yourself with the blame brush. The doctors said you *couldn't* have known. Josh's heart problem would have gone undetected until its inevitable failure. Do you remember that?"

"Yes, I remember." *But I was his mother, I should have known something was wrong.*

After several long moments of silence, the counselor said, "Are you sure about your decision to divorce your husband? It's all right to change your mind, you know."

Terri thought about it, searching through her confusion. Their marriage and the love between them had not been able to withstand the blow of Josh's death. It was broken, beyond her ability to repair. Now the only positive choice was to go on.

"I'm sure."

IT WAS after midnight when Terri finally took the elevator to the fourth floor. She'd look in on Michael one more time then go home to bed. She was beat. She waved to one of the night-shift nurses at the nurses' station, and pushed open the door to Michael's room.

The room was dim, lit only by the light leaking around the curtains from the streetlight outside.

Michael was asleep. She started to let the door swing closed and leave, when she heard his voice.

"Tam?" He sounded so odd, as if he was in pain.

A moment later, she was bending over him. "I'm here. What is it?"

He seemed to be dreaming. He moved his head, but his eyes were still closed.

"Tam!" The call was desperate.

"I'm here, Michael." A rush of adrenaline shot through her as she framed his face with her hands. His jaw was clenched and his skin felt too cool. She didn't know why, but she knew she had to wake him up, to bring him back, to save him from . . . from what? "Michael." She shook him slightly. "Wake up."

His eyes opened and he drew in a shuddering breath as his muscles relaxed. He didn't look at all surprised to wake up and find her there. It was almost as if he knew he'd called to her, and she'd come.

"Michael, what's going on? Should I call the doctor?"

His eyes glimmered in the dim light as he gazed at her. "The doctor can't help me," he said finally.

"What do you mean? He saved your life, he can—"

"The doctor didn't save me," he interrupted. "The angel did."

Terri stared at him, confused by his words. Was he still dreaming? Or, worse, still delirious? *Angels?* Michael had been raised a Catholic, but as far as she knew, other than on their wedding day and the day of Josh's funeral, he'd never set foot in a church as an adult. His religion had been the law and the court, his pulpit. "What did you say?" she asked, hoping for a different answer.

"The angel, he—"

"Michael." Terri lowered her face until her forehead touched his. Of all the things she'd thought might happen to him, the possibility of him losing his mind hadn't occurred to her. It would be more tragic than losing his life. "Oh, Michael, what happened to you out there?"

One of his hands covered hers as if he wanted to steady her before he answered.

"I died."

3

"YOU WHAT?" Terri asked.

Even though Michael couldn't see the doubt in her eyes, he could sense her withdrawal. The clear picture of her fear, her reluctance, as she edged away from him to turn on the fluorescent light above the bed, registered inside him.

"No," he said as he tugged her back. He didn't know how he could read her so well. God knows, he'd misread her often enough in the past. But since the storm and the angel, everything was different. Life had been distilled down to emotion, to the strongest connection between people. Maybe dying had finally taught him how to pay attention. Whatever the cause, he'd changed, and he could see no use in pretending otherwise. "I need to tell you what happened."

"It's dark in here. Let me—"

"The dark doesn't bother me anymore. And neither does death."

She hesitated. He knew he had her complete attention again, so he asked for what he wanted. It was suddenly very important for him to have her close. "Would you just sit next to me for a while?"

"Michael." His name, said in a tone that made her sound like a schoolteacher, made him smile. The familiar allure of her, the elemental, physical connection they'd always shared tugged at him.

"I'm in no shape to try anything beyond talking you to sleep," he said. "Please. I'd just like to hold your hand, and talk. Like you're my wife, not my nurse."

She was so still, he expected her to say no any second, and then walk away. He waited for what felt like an eternity, trying to recover that "knowingness" that he'd experienced before. But he only found confusion. His or hers, he couldn't tell. Finally, she turned and pulled a chair close to the side of the bed. He couldn't move his arm very far to touch her, but as their fingers entwined, the cool smoothness of her skin made him think of other times—times she'd touched him because she wanted to.

"Remember when we used to lie on the deck of the *Vanda* and look at the stars?"

"Tell me what happened out there." Her voice sounded strained, scared. Did she think he'd faced a man-eating shark or an alien from the Bermuda triangle? He'd only died. No big deal.

"I was . . . The storm." He stopped, then tried again, "You know the boat capsized." What had happened that day was crystal-clear in his mind. Why was he making such a mess of telling about it? "Something hit me in the head and I . . ." His memory drifted off into cold water, endless rain and wind. "I guess I drowned." He remembered one flash of panic that seemed ridiculous now. He passed it over as too inconsequential to mention. "I could see my body floating in the water and then the angel came."

The memory of the angel stood out like a fire in his mind. "So bright," he said, but he knew he couldn't describe the color or the quality of that light. Everything was gray in comparison. Except for his wife.

Terri seemed to have stopped breathing. He squeezed her hand to make sure he hadn't imagined her sitting next to him, that she wasn't some comforting vision his imagination had conjured out of the air.

"And we flew away through a tunnel of swirling clouds. So fast." Merely remembering made Michael's injured body feel lighter, freer. Again, he couldn't adequately describe the sensation. "No gravity. No time. Then I saw you."

"Me?" Terri's fingers tensed as though she'd been pinched.

"I saw my life, actually. Everything I've been and done. Josh . . ." Tears rose in his eyes and Michael was glad that he and Terri were in the dark. She'd never believe he was happy and sane if he cried like a six-year-old over seeing his dead son. "I, uh . . . you. You were laughing on our wedding day because I had arrived at the chapel two hours early with everything planned. But I didn't know I'd forgotten my shirt until thirty minutes before the ceremony. Do you remember? You had the keys to the apartment. I wasn't supposed to see you, so your sister nearly tackled me at the door. I thought you'd be mad.

"But you laughed." Michael drew in a deep breath, seeing her face in his mind once again. "You looked at me like I was the funniest, smartest, most important shirtless person in the entire universe . . . and you laughed."

Terri didn't move, but he felt something cool and wet fall on his arm. A tear. He hadn't meant to hurt her. He'd been trying to share his happiness. To tell her how much he wanted to be the man she thought he was on their wedding day. The man she'd loved—with or without a shirt. In an effort to lighten the emotion of the moment, he added, "If I hadn't already been dead, that look on your face would have killed me."

He got no response, so he stumbled on to the hard part, to the bad part. "Then I saw you the day Josh died." Michael felt Terri stiffen, and he had to swallow before he could say the words. "I saw the light go out in your eyes. Your anguish was so deep, so clear, I wanted to look away. But I couldn't, because at the time I had closed down, left you to struggle through it alone. And then, when you finally started to cry, you couldn't seem to stop. I thought it was my fault. And I ran from you, from our marriage, from Josh's death. This time, when I saw your tears, I had to face what I'd done.

"Then I saw Josh."

"Stop it." Terri couldn't take anymore. She pushed to her feet and pulled her hand out of his. "What are you trying to do, Michael?"

"Nothing. I mean, I'm trying to tell you what happened. How sorry—"

"Why do you want to bring it all up again?" Terri tried to concentrate on breathing normally. She thought she'd worked through her anger, but it only took a short time with Michael to bring it charging back. He'd deserted her, left her to wail at fate or at God for not helping her save her son. There had been nights when she would have begged

Michael to come back. To hold her, to talk to her, to love her until the pain and guilt went away. But she hadn't even known where he'd gone. Saying "I'm sorry" at this late date only made her furious.

"I want to try to make it up to you. To show you—"

"Don't, Michael." Terri tilted her head back to breathe, to fight the tears welling up in her eyes. She'd be damned if she'd cry in front of him now. "You can't make it up to me. If you need to talk to someone about Josh, then go to a counselor. That's how I managed to get through it." *Since I didn't have my husband,* her mind added. She moved away from the bed.

"Look, I know I didn't help you then, but I'm trying to help you now. I've seen—"

"You've seen the light. Is that it?" There was a wealth of bitterness in her voice. Then she had a terrifying thought—Michael could still make her angry. And she knew from counseling that anger meant feelings. He couldn't make her love him again? Could he?

She had to cling to the anger, to get out of here before she fell apart. "It's too late."

It couldn't be too late. Michael struggled with the impulse to get out of bed and charge after Terri as she left the room. He'd just gone about it wrong and she'd left him, alone in the dark with his apologies and his revelations. Physically, he knew he couldn't charge anywhere at the moment. His body needed time to heal. Maybe it would be best to give Terri a little more time, as well. He tried to picture how he must sound to her, how these changes inside him must seem to her, but he was too tired. Too emotionally drained. He could barely remember his own motivation from a week before. He only knew he was completely different now. Somehow, he had to prove that to his wife.

As he drifted through the half waking, half dreaming netherworld of sleep, however, the familiar sense of urgency tugged at his mind. The angel had brought him back to save Terri. To do something before . . . Michael fought sleep, trying to decipher the memory. The angel . . .

THE ANGEL SMILED.

Michael could feel his own features brightening. He knew he was grinning. Then he noticed the child who held the angel's hand.

Josh.

The expression of pure delight on Josh's face was enough to heal Michael's heart. One by one, each of the ragged ends of anguish inside him transformed into joy. Again, there were no actual words spoken. Michael simply looked at the angel and understood. Josh was fine, loved and watched over. And so happy to see his father that Michael could feel his son's love like a touch. Emotion rose inside him, and without thinking, he held out his hand and gestured for Josh to come to him.

Not yet. It's not your time.

Once more, Michael experienced that sense of urgency. He also felt a keen disappointment. He lowered his hand like a child who was offered a present then told he had to wait until Christmas morning. In this case, Michael knew he had to do something first. He had to save Terri. That's why he was alive.

The vision of the angel and Josh melted into the darkness and fear clouded Michael's joy. It was up to him, but he had to get Terri to trust him again. He couldn't save her if she didn't trust him.

"I THINK Michael is having some kind of breakdown," Terri said.

"Why do you say that?" Anna asked as she reluctantly poked her fork into the wilted salad before her on the table.

"Last night when I checked on him, he woke up and started talking about angels." Terri nearly choked on the words. "He said crazy things. That he saw me on our wedding day, that he saw Josh..."

Anna pushed the salad aside. "Maybe his life flashed before his eyes, like in a near-death experience. After all, he was almost dead when they brought him in."

"But he didn't flatline. Most near-death experiences happen to patients whose heart has stopped for a certain amount of time. No—" Terri shook her head slowly "—I think Michael has had a near-conscience experience. Either that, or the trauma to his head has knocked him off center. When he looks at me, I can see something in his eyes that I've never seen before. I don't know how to deal with it. Some of the things he says . . ."

"Did you mention it to Dr. Hubbard?" Anna asked, then snapped her fingers. "Or better yet, why don't you ask Tom Sizemore to stop in and talk to Michael? Maybe he could help."

Terri put down her coffee cup and shrugged. "I told Michael to see a counselor, but I don't know if Tom is the right one."

"At least he understands what happened to Josh and part of what happened to your marriage. Seems like a good idea to me."

A year ago, the night before he left, she'd been desperate to talk, or fight, or just cry in Michael's arms. But he hadn't given her the chance. Now, in self-preservation, she would have to insist that he talk to someone else. She'd gotten through her grief and made the decision to go on. Now Michael needed to do the same. "You're right. Maybe Tom could help. I'll ask him about it."

"What about you? How are you doing? Did you call to Dr. Perez?"

Terri sighed. "No. I've been so busy with Michael . . ."

"Terri . . ."

"I know, I know." She looked her friend in the eye. "I'm going to talk to Dr. Perez as soon as I get Michael squared away. Really."

"Well, I hope it's soon. I just heard about a great new restaurant, the Sandpiper, or the Sand Crab . . . something like that. Anyway, I figure that's the perfect place for us to celebrate your return to pediatrics."

Her *return* to pediatrics. Terri felt a shimmer of fear mixed with excitement. The same feeling that had been nagging her for some time now. Pediatrics had been her first love until she'd had a child of her own. After losing Josh, she'd been too hurt and too fragile to continue taking care of other people's children. But she was stronger now.

"So, what's so good about this restaurant?" she asked. "The food?"

Anna waved a hand in dismissal. "Oh, I don't know about the food, but I heard they have good-looking bartenders and they make a great drink called Sex on the Beach."

"Sounds dangerous," Terri said, smiling at Anna's outrageous logic.

"Hey, it's the safest sex a single working woman can have."

Terri shrugged as she pushed to her feet. "It's the only sex an ER nurse on the night shift is likely to have," she joked. Michael's image rose in her mind, the memory of his kiss, his body. She pushed it away. "I've got to get back. I'll let you know when to make the reservations."

"WELL, as difficult as it is to believe, I think we can let you out of here tomorrow," Dr. Hubbard said as he palpated Michael's chest with his fingers. Michael was sitting up on his own, and his skin, although peeling in patches from his sunburn, was a healthier color.

"Your ribs and shoulder are going to be tender for several weeks, but other than taking it easy, all you need is time." Dr. Hubbard turned to Terri. "He's going to need some care for the next few days, at least. Even getting dressed will be strenuous."

"Just a second," Terri interrupted. "Michael doesn't live with me. We're separated."

"I'm going home with you," Michael said.

The silence in the room was deafening. Terri drew in a long breath to fight the sinking feeling in her stomach. She remembered Michael's first words to her after regaining consciousness—"no divorce." She didn't know if he was playing a game, or if he'd lost his memory somewhere out there in the ocean. She only knew the time had come for her and Michael to have a serious talk.

"Would you excuse us for a few moments?" Terri asked Dr. Hubbard. She was amazed that her voice could sound so detached. She knew her hands were shaking.

"I have two more patients to see. If you have any questions, get one of the floor nurses to find me." The doctor dropped Michael's chart into its slot at the end of the bed and left the room.

Terri pushed the door closed after him and turned to face the man who was still legally her husband.

"Okay, Michael. What's going on?"

"Will you help me stand up? I need to go to the john."

Terri wasn't budging. "Why do you think I'll take you home with me?"

He looked at her with a confused and innocent expression that she didn't buy for a second. "You heard the doctor. I need someone to help me for a few days."

"Hire a nurse." Terri lost the calm, professional tone she'd worked so hard to acquire and her voice quivered. Something inside her was beginning to panic. She'd done her best to help him get well while he was in the hospital. Taking him home seemed above and beyond the call of duty.

Ever since he'd been delivered to the ER, she'd been forced to reexamine her hard-thought conclusions. She didn't want to get into her emotions. The less time they spent together, the better. As soon as Michael signed the divorce papers, and she appeared before the judge, their divorce would be final. Why was he so determined to force his way back into her life?

"Look, Terri." Michael's hazel eyes were level and rational. "I've been living on the boat. The boat is gone. Where else could I go? In the shape I'm in, I can't rent or buy a place to live." He sighed as if he'd hoped she would volunteer her house, legally, *their* house. "I'm only asking you to help me out for a few days—like any friend. We're still friends, aren't we?"

Terri forced herself to ignore the question and got back to the original issue—Michael and her living in the same house. A house full of the best and worst memories of her life. "You could check into the Holiday Inn."

He looked away and Terri wished for the millionth time that she could read his mind—just a little. But when he met her eyes again, he was as unreadable as ever. "I really don't want to be alone right now."

Terri watched him as she wrestled with her own disbelief and hurt. She hadn't wanted to be alone for the last year, but he'd disappeared. Why should she care whether he wanted to be alone now? She'd helped him recover. What else could she do?

Just say no, her logic ordered. *You've finally made the decision to divorce him and get on with your life. He may be confused, but don't let him confuse the issues.*

But Terri's heart knew what alone meant.

"Two days, Michael," she heard herself say. "That's it. And if you want to be waited on hand and foot, you'd better stay here. I have to work and—"

His smile stopped her words. His pirate smile, a little battered but still powerful. Terri swallowed against the sudden premonition that taking Michael home with her was a really bad idea.

Michael pushed aside the sheet covering him and gingerly slid his feet to the floor. He was naked except for boxer shorts and the rib splint. "Can you help me to the bathroom?"

Terri's gaze shifted from Michael's partially covered chest to his bare feet, and a surge of pure physical yearning shot through her. She'd always loved his body. During the happier days of their marriage, she'd made a point of getting to know it, inch by inch—scalp to toes. As she moved next to him and slipped an arm around his bare waist, she was jolted by the warm, familiar touch of his skin. Terri knew in that moment that her premonition was correct. Taking Michael home to stay with her was definitely a bad idea.

4

COMING HOME with Terri had been a good idea, Michael thought as he stared through the window of her Honda at the streets and buildings they passed. They drove down Flagler Boulevard with its stately royal palms running along the Intracoastal Waterway. It amazed him that the world looked the same as it had a week ago. He realized *he* was the one who had been irrevocably changed.

The downtown traffic of West Palm Beach remained a stop-and-go dance even though the tourist season didn't officially begin until after Christmas. The people who were always in a hurry to go somewhere continued their race. He was the only one who was different. The only one who had died.

Each block they passed seemed more familiar, yet to Michael, the familiar was now foreign. He didn't belong here. When the sun flashed off the chrome of the car in front of them, he thought of the ocean, of the angel, of seeing Josh. How had he chosen to return to the mundane comings and goings of living? Everything around him seemed less real, less important.

Everything but his wife.

When the person in the car behind them blew the horn, Michael looked over at Terri and smiled. She was the brightness, the reason he was glad to be alive, glad to be home.

Terri said something under her breath and looked away.

Finally, they turned into the neighborhood where he and Terri had lived as man and wife for five years—the historic El Cid section situated south of downtown and within a few blocks of the Intracoastal. Michael drew in a deep breath. Even the air smelled familiar. He remembered how excited Terri had been when they'd signed the real-estate contract. When they'd actually owned their first home.

They passed houses with sprinklers watering well-tended lawns. Terri waved to a man balanced on a ladder trimming an exora hedge that looked like an eight-foot-high green wall before turning into her driveway.

The house was typical of the old Spanish-style Florida homes built of block and stucco. From the sculpted, mission-style line of the roof along the front, to the sun porch on the back, it was a house built to enjoy the Florida weather. Thick, cool walls with lots of windows open to the breeze. Compared to the million-dollar-plus villas along the Intracoastal, this house was a cracker box . . . with a graceful past.

To Michael, it had simply been a good investment. And close to a good school for Josh. But after he'd made the slow, painful walk from the car, the open living room before him beckoned with a cool, flower-scented breeze that flowed through the floor-to-ceiling jalousie windows. And the wraparound couch that lined two walls of the room looked like heaven.

How many times had he made love to Terri on that couch? The memory, weighted by both pleasure and pain, reminded him of how much he wanted this second chance. Another chance to love Terri, to save her, to help her find some peace and happiness, even if she couldn't love him or trust him as she had before.

Michael slowly moved through the front door of their house. Her house, he corrected himself. It used to be their home. He hadn't missed the floor plan or the furniture, he'd missed the home Terri had made out of it. He was determined not to blow it again.

"Here," Terri said, appearing at his side and taking his arm. "Sit on the couch, and I'll get your stuff from the car."

Michael did as instructed. He needed to sit down. The nagging pain in his chest reminded him that he wasn't well yet. White phantoms seemed to dance in the corners of his vision.

He remembered what the angel had said, he had to save Terri. He'd gone over it again and again in his mind. Logically, in order to protect her, he needed to save their marriage. He had to show Terri that he'd changed, somehow convince her to trust him again. Then he would be there when she needed him. He had to make her see that the only reason for his being alive was that they were meant to be together.

Right now, he was in her home. A good beginning.

Sure. I'll stop by the office as soon as I feel better," Michael said into the phone. "Tell Marsh I appreciate the offer."

Terri felt like a rat for eavesdropping on the conversation, but she needed to know about Michael's state of mind, his plans. Especially his plans concerning her.

Due to the accident, she'd missed her appointment with the judge. And now, because of Michael's injuries, she didn't know how to bring up the subject. She'd taken the day off from the hospital to get him settled into the house, and from the sound of the conversation, he'd been offered the opportunity to rejoin the law firm he'd left more than a year ago. The whole scenario made Terri even more nervous. It was as if Michael had decided to put his old life back together again. To bring back the past step by step. And every so often, she would catch him staring at her. By the look in his eyes, she knew he'd included her in his plans.

But why? Why would he abandon her, disappear for over a year, then return as if nothing had happened? As if nothing had been missed.

He hung up the phone and tilted his head back to rest it against the couch. "I think I've about had it." He sighed. "I need to stretch out for a while." He made a feeble attempt to raise his feet and lie down.

"Let me help you into the bedroom. You'll be more comfortable on the bed than on the couch."

His eyes fluttered open, and he stared at her for a long time. "I'm so tired."

He looked tired, and pale. Fighting the twinge of alarm that ran through her at his uncharacteristic vulnerability, Terri set about helping him stand. She had to support a good deal of his weight as they slowly shuffled in a painful endurance test to the guest bedroom directly across the hall from her own. Halfway down the hall, Michael stumbled and had to lean against the wall for support.

Terry lightly balanced one hand on his chest as she waited for him to gather his strength. She could feel his heart pounding against the rib splint under his shirt. She was afraid that if she took her arm from around his waist, he would crumple to the floor. If he fell . . .

"Michael, you should have stayed in the hospital. The doctor would have—"

"No." His labored breathing gave his voice a harsh edge. "I'm better here with you. I'll be okay." He winced as he moved his foot forward. "I just need to rest a little."

He slept through dinner and the eleven o'clock news. Terri checked on him several times during the evening. His color was good and he seemed to be breathing all right. She finally went to bed around midnight.

As she stared at the shadows shifting across the ceiling, she wondered at the amazing events of the past several days. A week ago, if someone had told her that her almost ex-husband would be sleeping under her roof again, she would have told them they were nuts.

She had to be nuts to bring him here. She'd finally come to terms with the end of their marriage. She'd forced herself to stop loving Michael, to stop wanting him. She didn't intend to dredge up the grief and loneliness again. She wanted to get on with her life. To marry and...have children. Maybe then she would get over Josh's death, get over Michael's abandonment. But she'd never be able to start a new life if Michael thought he could barge into her house and back into her heart anytime he felt like it. If he thought that all he had to do was nearly get himself killed then snap his fingers—

"Tam?"

Terri's inner tirade skidded to a halt. She leaped out of bed, but stopped herself at the doorway of the guest room. Had Michael called her? Or had she been thinking about him so hard, she'd imagined it? She waited, listening to the sound of the wind rustling the palm trees near the window and to the pounding of her own heart.

Silence.

She quietly moved to the foot of the bed. Michael was asleep, not in pain, not calling her name. She shook her head at her own flight of fancy but stood transfixed. He had gotten the sheet twisted around one leg and pulled to the side. That left most of his chest and one leg bare. A sudden infusion of heat rose through Terri. She felt singed, remembering the long, lazy days on the boat. She'd never forgotten the way Michael had touched her, loved her. It had been so long since that day. . .

"You taste salty," Michael had mumbled into her hair before he'd again dipped his head to tease the side of her neck with his tongue.

Terri flinched as goose bumps rose along her sun-warmed skin. Michael was wet and dripping from a plunge in the ocean, but it wasn't the cold drops of water that caused the goose bumps. Her undivided attention had been caught by the cool weight of his hand splayed across her bare midriff.

"And you're so hot," he added, "I'm surprised you don't sizzle."

Terri opened her eyes then, but could only squint because of the bright morning sun beating down. Suddenly, his shadow fell across her face, and she could see him clearly. His dark brown hair was wet and slicked back except for a few heavy strands that fell forward. Drops of water on his tanned shoulders and chest glistened in the hot Florida sun. The playful gleam in his hazel eyes made something inside Terri flush and grow warm. He looked like a pirate, intent on having her for breakfast, lunch and dinner.

"You need to come in for a swim."

"You know I'm not wild about jumping off a boat in the middle of the ocean."

"First of all—" he shook his head to sprinkle her with drops of water "—we're not in the middle of the ocean. And second, if you don't get in the water or put on some sunscreen, you'll be cooked like a lobster." His lips teased hers lightly. "I have plans for this body and letting it get sunburned is not on the agenda."

His words sent another shiver of anticipation through her, but she covered it by playfully shoving his shoulder. "I'll put on some suntan lotion," she muttered. She rolled on her side and rummaged through the carryall bag she'd brought with her.

As soon as she'd pulled out the bottle, he grabbed it out of her hand. "Let me." His wicked smile made Terri's heart pound so hard she couldn't speak, much less argue. "It's a tough job, but somebody's got to do it. Turn over on your stomach."

The wet texture of his bathing suit was cool against the backs of her thighs as he straddled her. She felt a tug and the top of her suit loosened. Then his hands nearly spanned her waist and ran upward along her back. The smell of coconut surrounded her as Michael's hands slid across her skin.

She closed her eyes. Heaven is a boat, she thought dreamily, and having Michael's hands on her.

His palms traveled along her ribs, fingers just brushing the sides of her breasts. *"Michael."* Terri wasn't able to wait anymore. When his hands started upward for another pass, she arched her back, silently begging him to touch her, to cup her. His hands, slick with the lotion, devastated her.

"Is this what you want?" His voice still had a playful tone but it sounded forced.

Terri experienced a rush of tingling pleasure when his hands covered her breasts, slicking them with the oil. She sucked in a sharp breath and answered him honestly. "Yes." She dropped her forehead on her crossed arms and surrendered to the slow-handed pleasure of Michael's touch.

He systematically coated her body with lotion from her throat to her toes, shucking her bathing suit in the process. By the time he'd come to be naked beside her, Terri's skin seemed to be on fire . . . and not from the sun.

Michael bracketed her face between his hands and looked into her eyes. That's when she noticed that his hands were trembling. "Let's make a baby," he whispered.

She wasn't able to speak, but nodded yes in answer to his suggestion.

"Tam." His voice was hoarse and all signs of playfulness had disappeared. "Tam, I—" His mouth covered hers with new urgency, and Terri gave herself over to the feelings, to the man she was crazy about. To her husband.

Heaven is a boat, her heart had whispered, *a bright Florida day. . . and Michael.*

That day was indelibly carved into her memory. The dip and roll of the ocean beneath the boat, the sun and the smell of coconut . . . and Michael.

Tears rose in Terri's eyes, and she realized she was gripping the bed frame with both hands. Slowly, she regained her sense of the present and pulled the tatters of her anger around her like a cloak. No one had ever made her feel the way Michael had, and possibly, no one ever would. He knew exactly how to touch her and how to make her wait. Her eyes traveled along his familiar, shadowed form.

And she still wanted him.

Even though she'd put her love away. . . . No matter how much pain had passed between them, the thought of his mouth on her skin, his hands . . . the feel of him inside her . . . still made her knees weak. She wished . . .

Fear choked off the pleasant memories. Terri caught herself and slowly backed away from the bed, then turned toward her own room. Wanting

Michael was too dangerous, and she'd forced herself to stop loving him. She couldn't afford the price. Terri retreated to the bed she'd shared with Michael before Josh's death, before their lives and their marriage had been shattered. Nothing would ever be the same again. Wishing couldn't change that. . . .

5

SHE'D MOVED all his clothes.

Michael stared into the open closet, alternating between relief that she'd kept anything of his, and annoyance at having been systematically relegated out of Terri's life. His suits were neatly arranged, covered by plastic. His shirts were clean and pressed. But his clothes didn't belong in the guest room, they belonged next to Terri's in the master-bedroom closet. Just as he belonged next to Terri in their king-size bed.

He couldn't blame her. He'd walked out the door without looking back. Afraid to look back to see the suffering he'd caused. And all those empty months spent alone on the boat, he'd thought he'd done the right thing . . .

One step at a time, Michael reminded himself as he made the slow, painful trip down the hall. He needed coffee—right now. When he shuffled between the living room and the Florida room, he found Terri. Dressed in a loose T-shirt with a rainbow emblazoned on the front and a pair of cotton running shorts, she sat on the couch, one bare leg curled beneath her, reading the newspaper.

She glanced up, startled. "Do you need help?" she asked. She slipped off her reading glasses and tossed them on the folded newspaper before she stood up. "I didn't hear you. I thought you were still asleep."

Michael fought the smile that tugged at his mouth. He wanted to tease her about her reading glasses the way he always had in the past, but she didn't look in the mood for teasing. "I could really use some coffee."

She moved toward him looking concerned that he might fall over at any moment, but didn't take his arm as she'd done the day before. "Sit down. I'll get you some." She watched him make his way to the couch before she disappeared around the corner. "Still take it with cream only?" she called from the kitchen.

"Right," he replied.

She returned and handed him a steaming cup that smelled of coffee and hazelnuts.

"I thought I'd let you sleep as long as you needed," she said. "How do you feel?" Her voice sounded as professional as that of any of the nurses at the hospital. Any minute, he expected her to take his pulse.

"Much better, actually." Experimentally, he raised his uninjured left arm and flexed it. "Still sore as hell," he grumbled. He didn't try the right arm. No sense pushing his luck. The strain of getting out of bed and into a loose pair of sweatpants had nearly taken his breath away. He watched as Terri's gaze traced over his shoulders then downward along his chest and the rib splint. A slight blush tinted her skin and a new thought occurred to him.

"I'd give anything for a long, hot shower." His sunburned skin was still sensitive, but in some spots he'd begun to peel, and the itching was driving him crazy. He plucked at the rib splint with his good hand. "Do you think you could help me out of this getup and into the shower?"

Terri looked as though she'd rather swallow her tongue. She took a long time to think it over. "I'm not sure that's a good idea," she answered finally.

"A little water won't hurt me. I floated around in the ocean for three days and I'm still—"

"I'll fix some breakfast first," she interrupted, then disappeared into the kitchen again.

Michael smiled then. The prospect of a shower was pleasant enough. The thought of a shower with Terri's help, with Terri's hands touching him made parts of his body go on red alert. It had been so long. And he wanted her to touch him in any and every way.

"Do you want scrambled or fried?"

Michael abruptly came back to reality. At that moment, *he* felt scrambled and fried. "Whatever you're having," he managed to call out and hoped that in the not too distant future, she'd be having him.

"IT'S NOT LIKE you've never seen me naked before," Michael complained in the tone of a disgruntled child. He'd been ordered to face the wall as she stripped off his boxer shorts.

"I'm not interested in seeing you naked today," Terri replied as she efficiently wrapped a towel around his waist and tucked it in securely. She turned him around and took his arm to help him step into the shower, then stepped in after him. "Now, sit down on the stool."

"This is no fun."

Terri moved around behind him and adjusted the water temperature. As she faced his bare back with the hand-held shower attachment, she wondered if she should make the water temperature a lot colder. "Do you want fun? Or do you want a shower?"

"I want a shower, but I—"

A blast of warm water on the back of his neck stopped his words. He sighed and let his head fall forward. Terri almost sighed, too. She was suffering from a variety of sensations—reluctance, longing, caution—and didn't know how to act. So she shifted into automatic. Helping Michael as she'd always helped him, but impersonally. She moved the spray from his neck and shoulders to his hair, and rubbed her hand through the dark strands. His face was obscured by running water but the texture of his hair under her palm, the warmth of the water and his skin . . .

"Here—" she tapped his good arm with the sprayer "—hold this." Michael rested the nozzle on his knee with the spray aimed at his chest. Terri poured a dollop of shampoo into her hand and rubbed it into his hair. "Put your head back and close your eyes." Michael did as instructed. As Terri worked the shampoo into a lather, she tried to keep her mind blank. To treat Michael as she would any other hospital patient. Instead of looking down at the blissful expression on his face, she focused on counting the tiles in the shower stall. On the annoying fact that her shorts and the front of her T-shirt were getting soaked. She couldn't think of how it felt to be sliding her fingers through Michael's shampoo-slick hair. Of how, in only moments, her hands would be moving over his skin.

"Ouch!" Michael opened one eye and frowned at her.

Terri realized she'd forgotten his head injury and unconsciously had tightened her grip along with her defenses. "Sorry." She reached over his shoulder for the sprayer. A moment later, shampoo suds cascaded down Michael's back and chest as she rinsed his hair. She returned the sprayer to him and picked up a washcloth and soap, then moved around to stand between his knees.

"Face first." She glanced down at him. He looked worried.

"What's wrong?" she asked as she lathered the cloth.

"Oh, I don't know. I sort of feel like a dog who's been out in the mud and now I'm about to get the bejesus scrubbed out of me. Remember, I'm an injured man."

Terri stifled the urge to smile. She pulled her gaze away from his for a close inspection of his face. One side had been sunburned pretty badly and remained pink in patches. The swelling in his lips and eyes had nearly disappeared. But overall, he looked thinner. He'd lost the well-fed-lawyer look and gained a few squint lines at the corners of his eyes. She thought again how lucky he was to be alive. "Don't worry, I'll try not to hurt you."

She raised his chin and he closed his eyes. He hadn't shaved in nearly a week and the slight blurring the whiskers gave to his strong jawline made him look even more of a stranger. Dangerous. A naked pirate in her husband's skin. Her ex-husband, to all intents and purposes. Terri brought her thoughts back under control and carefully washed and rinsed his face before she stepped back.

"Okay, stand up."

"Can I get rid of this towel now?" Michael asked as he stood. "It's not really hiding anything."

Terri's eyes lowered to the towel before she recognized her mistake. The wet weight of the thick cloth only accentuated the shape of his erection.

"I may be injured, but I'm not dead."

The urge to playfully run her hand over that straining hardness hit her like a shock wave. How many nights had she spent tossing and turning alone in their king-size bed wishing she could touch him? With a groan and a glare, Terri turned him away from him so she could avoid his knowing gaze.

When Terri began to scrub his back, Michael nearly groaned. God, it felt so good. And he felt so alive. If his chest and shoulder didn't ache as though he'd been hit by a truck, he'd turn around and convince Terri that he hadn't forgotten how to make her moan. Over the years of their marriage, he'd made it a point to find out just what his wife liked sexually. What drove her over the edge. God, he loved to tease her and touch her and push her until she was half-crazy.

Being so close to her now, with that damp T-shirt clinging to the heavy shape of her breasts, and her skin dewy from the steam, made him hurt in places that weren't injured. He wanted to kiss the wet strands of hair clinging to her neck and taste her sweet skin with his tongue. He wanted to make love to her for the next twelve hours or so. However long it took to erase the wary look of distrust in her eyes. The look he'd put there by running away.

Terri's fingernails lightly scraped the skin somewhere near his spine and Michael felt like swearing. If he only had the strength to hold her still for a few moments, he knew at least three things he could do that would make her forget everything except his mouth and hands.

Terri watched her own fingers slip through the soapy bubbles on Michael's broad, tanned back as if her hand belonged to someone else. She couldn't think about what she was doing. She had to keep moving and get this over with. If she stopped to think, she would . . . enjoy this too much.

Then another thought assailed her. Michael had been living on his boat for the last year. Sailing from place to place, island to island. Had he been alone? Or had some other woman admired his back, run her hands over his skin, felt him inside her?

The picture of that possibility filled Terri's mind, and her heart clenched in reaction. Immediately, her well-rehearsed logic came to the rescue. *No!* She didn't want to know. Their marriage was over. She'd made up her mind. She didn't love him anymore. All that remained was the formality of legally finalizing the divorce.

Forcing herself to deal with the issue at hand, she grasped Michael's biceps and turned him toward her, pushing the soapy cloth under his arm then across his chest. Then she made the mistake of looking into his eyes.

The blatant desire in his gaze caused her hand to pause in midmotion and nearly stopped her heart. With unhurried movements, he pulled the cloth out of her grasp, dropped it onto the stool, then pressed her slippery palm against his chest—skin to skin.

"Tam...please touch me...I've missed you so."

Terri watched him lean toward her and felt her own chin rise to meet his mouth. The sound of his voice, close and intimate, the texture of his wet skin beneath her fingers sank below the surface of her grief and regret. She had to kiss him, to taste him just once more. All those nights she'd had to get through without him tightened her throat and tunneled into one thought. He was real and alive and standing before her. She *had* to kiss him. She had to know if he still . . .

His lips were wet and warm and oh-so-familiar. Every erotic memory of what his mouth was capable of rushed through her. The spray of water pattered against the wall of the shower and steam rose around them. His whiskers prickled against her skin as he shifted the angle, deepened the kiss. His tongue teased her lips wider, and Terri felt lost and found at the same time.

Michael.

Michael's fingers twisted the side of her T-shirt and pulled her forward. He wanted to feel her body against his—to get inside her clothes. He wanted to hold her the way he had before their lives had been broken. Before Josh. When Terri had still loved him, still trusted him.

Tam.

The sweet pleasure of her mouth and her breasts touching his chest made Michael's head foggy. How had he stayed away from her for so long? He needed his wife. Now. Whether she loved him or not. He would show her how good they were together, love her until she smiled again.

He raised his right arm to hold her, to pull her closer—and paid the price. Pain like the thrust of a sword tore through his chest and shoulder. He couldn't stop an involuntary gasp.

Terri pulled back as if she were the one who'd hurt him. Her lips were moist and parted, her skin flushed with the warmth he'd ignited. Her wet shirt clung and clearly outlined the hard buds of her nipples begging for his touch. As Michael panted and waited for the ache to subside, he watched her expression change from dazed pleasure to alarm. She pressed shaking fingers to her lips as if she couldn't believe what had just happened.

"Tam?"

Shaking her head, she took one step backward, then turned, stepped out of the shower and nearly ran from the room.

6

HE FOUND HER in the orchid house.

After finishing his shower as best as he could alone, Michael had shaved using his electric razor and had gotten dressed again. The house seemed so quiet and empty, he thought Terri had left. But then he'd seen the back door ajar and followed the stepping stones across the yard to the orchid house.

As he stepped into the cool shade provided by the wooden slats and netting stretched over the roof, a strong sense of déjà vu assailed him. He remembered nailing every wooden slat in place, planning the best way to fit the shelves needed for the pots of orchids, trying to figure out the eight billion tiny parts of an automatic watering system. Without conscious thought, his left hand rose to realign one of the supports for the door frame. He'd intended to fix that someday. Someday.

Terri stood at the opposite end of the enclosure poised in the act of misting some of the plants. She'd changed out of her wet clothes and was wearing a blouse and a pair of walking shorts.

Cool, comfortable and remote, she looked at him warily. For that fleeting space in time, he could physically feel the confusion in her, the aftermath of arousal. The sensation was too strong and too clear not to be true and it surprised him once again. Was this a new talent he'd acquired by dying or was this feeling, this *knowing*, simply a hallucination?

"Are you okay?" he asked.

"I'm fine," she answered, then continued misting the orchids closest to her. She wasn't fine, and he wasn't going anywhere.

"I'm not sorry," he said.

"What?"

Michael walked toward her, absently admiring the different colorful blooms on some of the orchids. A memory like a snapshot flashed through his mind—he and Josh picking out a new plant for Terri on Mother's Day. *Mother's Day...* He stopped at the end of the row and looked at her again. "I'm not sorry I kissed you. I want you so much—"

"Michael..."

"No. Don't Michael me. We need to talk."

She clutched the spray bottle as if she needed a weapon, and Michael sensed her fear like a wall between them. "Talking can't change anything."

"Yes, it can." He sighed in exasperation. "Something has to. I've changed and I know things can be different between us." He took one more step toward her, searching for a way to break through. "Look, I'm not sure why I left other than the fact that I couldn't face you. I couldn't look into your eyes and see the pain about Josh, the pain that I thought I'd caused.

"But now I know it wasn't my fault. The angel fixed something in me. I came back and I need to stick around for a while, to help you find some peace and happiness."

Terri set the bottle on the plant shelf next to her. She looked bleak and resigned and it made Michael's chest hurt. "I never blamed you for what happened to Josh." She turned away from him and picked up a cloth to wipe her hands. "And you're right, you have changed. I can see that. But, I've changed, too. It won't do either of us any good to hang on to the past, to the way things used to be."

"Some things are still the same," Michael said. "When you touch me . . . kiss me, I—"

"That shouldn't have happened," Terri interrupted as her gaze shifted to his. She slowly drew in a breath. He watched the muscles in her throat shift as she swallowed and he braced himself.

"Our marriage is over. Do you remember? A month ago you sent a message through Marsh that you would sign the divorce agreement. I'm holding you to that. And, I think you should talk to a counselor."

"You think I've lost it?" In the past, Michael had been used to listening to his own advice. Now he was listening to an angel's. Did that make him crazy in Terri's eyes?

"Does it matter what I think? We both have had good reasons to lose it. Our marriage, our . . . love wasn't strong enough to get us through the grief together. You did what you had to do and I lived through it." Her fingers curled inward, gripping the cloth in a fist. "Right now, I'm holding on with my fingernails, and every time you bring up the past, you bring back the heartache. I don't deserve that— not from you."

He wanted to put his arms around her and convince her. To get her to look at the world through his eyes, through the angel's words. But he knew mere words wouldn't do it. And right now, that's all he had. "I don't want to hurt you," he said, meaning it more than he'd ever meant anything in his life.

"Then let it go. Let the past go. Let me go."

"WELL, that was number twenty-eight. Is it a full moon, or what?" Anna pulled back the curtain on the now-empty treatment room and stripped off her rubber gloves.

Terri smiled and glanced at her watch. Traffic in the emergency room always increased on holidays and during a full moon. And they'd been busy all evening. Her shift had ended an hour ago, but she couldn't make herself leave. At work, she knew who she was and what had to be done. At home, with Michael, since he'd kissed her—

"Isn't it time for you to hit the road?" Anna asked.

"Yeah." Terri tried to sound nonchalant. "But I'm in no hurry. When is your dinner break?"

Anna stopped and stared at her friend. "You know, if you really can't face going home when he's there, you ought to throw him out."

Terri shrugged and gave up trying to hide her confusion. It had been over twelve hours since Michael had kissed her, but she hadn't recovered. It would be a lie to say she hadn't felt anything, that she didn't want him. "Easy for you to say. You're not still married to him."

"No, and neither are you, really. What's happening with the judge?"

"I have to call about setting another court date for the final judgment. But I can't until Michael is well enough."

They walked down the corridor in the direction of the nurses' station. "How is he?" Anna asked.

"Better." Terri thought of how Michael's pain had saved her from his kiss, from herself. "He walks well enough but he can only raise his right arm a few inches." And she intended for him to be out of her house before he fully recovered. Otherwise, she'd have no protection from him, or from the sparks that had ignited between them from the beginning. It wasn't fair, Terri fumed. If Michael were a stranger, she'd have no trouble resisting the sensual pull. She wouldn't *know* how good it could be.

"Is he planning to stay in West Palm?" Anna asked as she moved behind the counter and headed for the office.

Terri hesitated as an uncomfortable thought caught her attention; Michael living in West Palm again. It was one thing to cut him out of her life after he'd already deserted her; but it was quite another to live in the same city, to know that she could see him if she wanted. To wonder who might take her place in his life. Or worse, to run into him occasionally and see him happily escorting another woman . . . or another wife.

When he'd followed her into the orchid house, Terri's first thought had been to resist the physical attraction. But something completely different had frightened her. Something so simple. With one tiny action, Michael had transformed himself into the loving husband she'd missed so desperately. When he'd reached up and pushed the doorframe back into place, as he had done every single time he'd walked through the door he'd built for her with his hands, with his love, she'd realized just how much they had lost.

Everything. But in that moment, she'd seen a tiny glimpse of Josh in his father's face, and she'd wanted to put her arms around him and welcome him home. To ask him to stay and to see if they could find that love again; the caring, the simplicity of the past. She'd longed for all of it. The love...

Anger filled her, along with hopelessness. She'd spent months coming to grips with the past and ended up with the only sane conclusion—to move forward. She couldn't go back. Michael's abandonment had nearly destroyed her. Their happiness—their marriage—was dead. As dead as their son.

MICHAEL OPENED his eyes feeling as if someone had touched him. He'd fallen asleep on the couch but now, suddenly, he was wide-awake. He rolled to one side and looked toward the clock on the VCR. It read eleven-thirty. Terri would be home any minute from the hospital. That should have been a comforting thought, but Michael couldn't shake the feeling that something was wrong.

Thirty minutes later, he was up, pacing a path between the living room and the Florida room, trying to get himself under control. Where was she? How could he keep her safe if he couldn't even drive a car? Any number of things could happen between the hospital and home. He stopped pacing and stared at the phone. He could always take a cab to the hospital and ride home with her. He picked up the phone book to find the number of the hospital.

"YOU WANT to talk about it?"

Terri didn't need to turn around. She recognized Tom Sizemore's voice. The fact that he was still working so late didn't surprise her. Grief kept its own hours. And, unlike her husband, Tom had always been there for her. He moved up next to her and stared out in the same direction.

Instead of going home to Michael, she'd come up to the roof of the hospital to breathe and to think. To be alone. There *was* a full moon and a breeze coming off the ocean, over the Intracoastal. Terri turned her face into the wind.

"Do you believe in angels, Tom?"

There was a stretch of silence as the counselor chose his words. "I believe in God, and I suppose that includes angels."

"No. I mean guardian angels...who watch over us."

After another careful silence, he said, "I'd like to believe in them. But I can't say that I do."

Terri looked at him. "So you classify angels under wishful thinking?"

"Well, it depends on the circumstances. Some schizophrenics speak to angels on a regular basis. That's a little more than wishful thinking." He smiled slightly. "Why this sudden interest in angels? Did you read a book or see a television program about them?"

Terri shifted her gaze away from Tom's. "No, it's Michael. He says he saw an angel when he was lost out in the ocean." She waited for a comment but Tom remained silent. "He said the angel saved his life and fixed something in him."

"Really? Do you believe him?"

Terri sighed. "I don't know. It sounds crazy, but he's so different. *Something* changed him. It's unnerving when he looks at me. Like he can read my mind or something. And he's so peaceful. Like he understands Josh's death and can let it go.

"I'd like to believe in angels if they would give me a little of that peace," Terri added.

"We all face grief in our own way. You've done pretty well on your own—without any illusions or quick answers."

"I thought so. I thought I had talked my way through it—figured it out. But I haven't found any peace. Does it ever get easier?"

"Yes, and no." He turned to face her, leaned against the retaining wall and crossed his arms. "Time helps, but we have to learn to look to the present and the future for our happiness, not the past. Not even to angels." He looked down for a moment and scuffed his toe along the gravel of the roof. "You know, when, Cheryl—um . . . my wife died, I expected the suffering, the grief. I let it run me until time cushioned the blow. Then I used it to get through school, to become a counselor. But what I didn't expect was what came after the grief—fear."

Terri turned and he met her eyes with a steady gaze. "I was afraid to be happy. To be peaceful. To trust life enough not to hurt me again."

His words mirrored the darkness inside her. She had to look away. The lights reflected on the water blurred as Terri's eyes filled with moisture. She was afraid. Of the future, of herself, of Michael. How could she even think of taking him back into her life? Of loving him again? No matter how different he seemed.

"Living in the pain I already knew felt safer than trying again. Deciding to go on is a very brave and scary thing."

"How did you do it?" Terri managed to say as she blinked back the tears and sniffed.

Tom's smile was equally sad and rueful. "I'm not sure I have done it. But I'm finally willing to try."

"I thought I was going on until Michael showed up. But now..." *That she'd kissed him*, she finished silently.

"Now?"

She shook her head and looked back out over the water. How could her heart trick her so cruelly? She knew that she couldn't depend on Michael. What masochistic part of her wanted to volunteer to be a fool again—a fool who believed in his angel?

A fool who would ultimately end up alone.

"I'm so confused. I've made new friends, decided on a step-by-step plan for the future. Yet right now, starting my life over looks like more than I can manage." She put her hands on the low wall and leaned over to stare down at the street below. Losing Josh had left an empty place inside her that nothing could fill. The idea of giving up was so seductive. One small step over the edge could end the anguish, give her peace. "It would be a lot easier to fly off this roof than to have to make decisions, to be strong." She glanced at Tom again. "To be brave."

"Is that why you came up here?"

Terri sighed as all the fear and anger drained out of her. It was after midnight. She was tired and she wanted to go home. "No. You know I'm too practical to be suicidal. Besides, I've seen too many people come into the ER who've tried and failed. I don't need any more problems."

"Good, because it looks bad on my record to have clients jumping off the roof."

A small, sad smile rose inside her. "Who knows, maybe Michael's angel would save me, too." She patted Tom's arm as she turned to go downstairs. "Or maybe the angel just sent you in its place."

WHEN THE ELEVATOR doors opened on the first floor, Michael stood on the other side. He was wearing sweatpants, tennis shoes with no laces or socks, and a loose, colorful shirt she would have called Hawaiian if they hadn't been in Florida.

In happier days, she might have teased him about being a fugitive from the fashion police, but these weren't happier days and he looked alarmed, as though it had been announced on the news that the hospital was under siege.

"Where have you been? Your shift ended over two hours ago."

"Michael? What in the world are you doing here?"

"I was worried about you. I—" His words stopped as his gaze locked on Tom Sizemore.

"Tom Sizemore, this is my . . . husband, Michael Weldon," Terri said. The two men nodded to acknowledge the introduction since Michael couldn't shake hands. "Tom is my Employee Assistance counselor."

Michael didn't appear very relieved. "What's wrong?" he asked.

"Nothing, I—" Terri looked toward Tom, searching for words.

"Listen, I have to check in with my service." He touched Terri's arm. "Call if you need me." Then he turned to Michael and hesitated, long enough to make Terri wonder what he might say about her, and the roof. Or about angels. "Nice to meet you," he said finally. A moment later, he was gone.

Terri made an assessing examination of Michael and realized he looked about ready to collapse. She took his good arm and turned him around. "Come over here and sit down. You look awful."

Michael sat on a padded bench in the corridor, leaned his head back and closed his eyes. He took several calming breaths.

Terri pressed her fingers to the side of his neck. "Are you dizzy? Do you want to lie down?"

"No. I'm fine." A sigh escaped him. He opened his eyes but didn't move. "Where were you?" His question didn't sound angry or accusing. It sounded confused.

"The ER was really busy tonight so I stayed a little longer. I thought you'd be asleep."

"I couldn't sleep. I knew you needed me."

His words put the brakes on Terri's concern. "What do you mean?"

"I'm not sure . . . I just knew."

She withdrew her hand from his neck. How had he known that she needed someone to talk to tonight? That she was feeling confused and afraid? Balanced on the edge of a breakdown. After all the times she'd wanted him, nights she'd cried because he wasn't there. Why did he finally get it when it was too late? "I've lived alone for over a year. Why are you so worried about me now?"

"Look—" Michael sat up straighter and ran his left hand through his hair "—that was then and this is now. I want to worry about you. The angel said I have to—"

"The angel?" Terri interrupted. Where was Tom when she needed him? She felt like shaking her fist at the sky. "Michael, there aren't any angels." *If there were, one would have saved Josh.* "You've had a head injury and you—"

"You're wrong."

Terri closed her eyes and mentally began to count. She hoped that by the time she got to ten, she'd know what to say. Anna's voice stopped her at five.

"Terri? Do you need some help?"

Terri opened her eyes, then glanced sideways at Michael. "No. We're all right," she answered. She knew she didn't sound very convincing. Michael remained silent. She pushed to her feet and bent to take his good arm. "Let's go home."

Michael swayed slightly as he stood and frowned. Then he looked at Anna. "Have you got any aspirin in this place?"

"For you, I can probably scare some up."

They walked down the corridor and through the ER where Anna produced the aspirin and a cup of water. Terri left Michael waiting with Anna at the emergency entrance while she made the hike to the parking lot to get the car.

MICHAEL'S HEAD pounded, but he needed to talk. Terri hadn't said a word since she'd helped him fasten his seat belt. He had to start somewhere.

"I know you think I'm crazy, but—"

"I don't think you're crazy," Terri interrupted. "I think you're confused and hurt, and you need some time to get back to normal."

He thought about that for a moment. All of it was true but there was more. Why couldn't he just tell her? Tell her what? That she might die? And that the thought terrified him because the angel had told him he was the only one who could save her? Instead of filing a petition for divorce, she'd probably file papers to have him committed. So, he took the middle of the road. "I'm supposed to look out for you. That's what the angel said."

"And that's why you came to the hospital tonight?" She still sounded skeptical.

"Yes."

"If something happened to me at the hospital, there are any number of professionals there to help me—from nurses to security. What could you do in your condition?"

"I don't know. I just woke up and knew something was wrong. I had to get to you." He'd felt that sense of urgency again, as clear as a call.

Terri went silent, seeming to concentrate solely on driving. Michael searched around inside for the right words. The ones that came out surprised him.

"I sailed the boat into that storm on purpose."

Gooseflesh tingled along Terri's arms as a chill ran through her. "What?" She needed a moment, a time-out. Her own ambivalence about being a survivor was too fresh in her mind.

He turned to look at her. "I wanted to die."

"I can understand that," she said, resisting the pull of his gaze.

"You can?"

"Yes. I know the feeling," Terri said, hanging by a thread to her calm demeanor. Her throat felt tight. She wanted to scream at him like a madwoman. Josh's death had taken part of her heart, Michael's desertion had wounded what was left. If he'd ended his life, out there on the ocean, alone, she wasn't sure she could have held on to her sanity for one more hour, one more day. She didn't want to feel sorry for him, to share his agony. She didn't want to know that he would rather have died than come back home to her. "You almost got what you wanted. You almost died."

"But I came back for you."

She looked at him then, she couldn't help it. She'd hoped, and prayed, and waited over a year for him to come back. But he hadn't. And then she'd filed for divorce. Now it was too late to believe in his excuses, his words, his pain. Too late to trust this changed man who wore her husband's face.

Peripherally, Terri saw that the light at the intersection they were approaching had changed to red. She pulled her gaze back to the road and hit the brake pedal a little too hard. She heard Michael's intake of breath at the slight jolt against the seat belt. The man in a car coming in the other direction blew his horn at them and made an angry gesture.

Terri's heartbeat fluttered faster. "Sorry," she breathed as she looked at Michael again. The frown on his face transformed into a slight smile.

"I don't particularly want to die tonight, though. I have a few more things to do." He watched her as if he could see the panicked thoughts in her head. As if he could tell that listening to his confession or knowing anything about what he wanted to do would hurt her too much. Then, his concentration shifted, wandered. He'd obviously reached the limit of his energy. He leaned his head back and closed his eyes. "You drive. I'll shut up. That way, we'll both make it home alive."

The light turned green and Terri touched the gas pedal, keeping her eyes on the road before her, and her thoughts away from the man beside her. The stranger who was her husband.

7

MICHAEL WOKE UP first. As he went through the slow, painful ritual of dressing, he listened to the birds chirping and calling outside the window, getting on with their day. When he lived on the boat, he'd rarely slept late. The sun seemed to come up faster over the ocean, bright and insistent. Then the raucous seabirds, or the wind, or the other boats anchored close by would begin their day, and he would follow suit. Already, his life on the boat seemed indistinct, condensed into one long dream. He did remember one thing, however, about the sun coming up and the world going on. Every single morning, he'd awakened missing Terri.

Now, the stillness inside the house surrounded him. With only a slight change in his breathing pattern, he pushed to his feet and stepped into the hall. Terri's bedroom door was half-open and he couldn't resist the urge to look in.

Still asleep. As he watched, she restlessly turned and pushed her face into the pillow. Maybe she knew it was time to get up but was refusing the knowledge, he thought. He wished he could walk over and slip under the sheets next to her. To feel her unguarded and soft in his arms, to smell her sweet unique, feminine perfume. He would wake her up slowly with gentle, good-morning kisses and slow, teasing touches. He would make her want to open her eyes and smile. His body reacted to the image and before he realized what he was doing, he had pushed open the door and taken a step into the room.

The framed photograph on the bed stand stopped him. Josh's picture, an old one, when he was two or three. The only thing in the house that she'd kept close to remind her of her son. Gone was the family portrait that used to occupy that space. Michael looked around the room—no other memories. Nothing of him. It was as if he'd never existed. He backed away, reminded again that he wasn't welcome in Terri's life, in her bed. And it was his own fault.

Slowly, he made his way down the hall to the kitchen. One step at a time. Jumping into bed with Terri wouldn't solve the problems between them, even if it would make them both feel better.

After making coffee, he wandered outside to the connected garage. His BMW was sitting exactly as he had parked it a year before. He thought of raising the garage door and trying to start it, but he wasn't sure he could manage to get in and turn the key without pain. Besides, the battery was probably dead, and even if it wasn't it would make too much noise. After the amount of time she'd spent taking care of him in the hospital, he figured Terri could use all the sleep she could get.

When he returned to the kitchen, however, he heard the shower running in the master bath.

TERRI HADN'T slept well. She'd dreamed of work, of rushing around the ER looking for something and not being able to find it. She'd woken up more tired than when she'd gone to bed and decided she needed a nice hot shower to help her wake up. Unfortunately, memories of washing Michael's hair and scrubbing his back intruded on her pleasure.

She stepped out of the shower and opened the door to release some of the steam. The welcome odor of coffee drifted to her on the cooler air. She spied a fresh cup sitting on the dresser beside the bathroom door. Terri peeked into the room before she opened the door wider. She wasn't sure she could handle another naked confrontation with Michael. Finding the room empty, she gratefully retrieved the coffee and took a sip. It had been a long time since someone had made her coffee in the morning. One of those little things that people who live together take for granted. She'd been alone long enough to miss it.

She'd finished the coffee by the time she'd dried her hair and gotten dressed. Her thoughts were on breakfast as she moved down the hall to find Michael.

He was sitting at the kitchen table with the phone book open and the phone in his hand. His gaze roamed over her from head to foot as he watched her walk into the room.

"Sure," he said into the phone. "I'll stop by there. That would be great if you can put a rush on it." He smiled at her and clamped his fingers over the receiver. "Good morning," he said. Then he ended the phone conversation. "Okay, bye."

"Hi," she replied and started to walk past him to get more coffee. But she stopped. "Thanks for making the coffee," she said.

"You're welcome. It's one of the few things I can do one-handed."

Terri thought of the shower, and of some of the things he hadn't been able to do and busied herself pouring herself another cup of coffee. She quickly changed the subject. "I'll make us something for breakfast."

"How about taking an invalid out for breakfast?" When she didn't answer right away he added,

"I'll buy. I need to go by the bank and withdraw some money and order new checks. Mine went down with the boat."

Better for their time together to be spent out in public than home alone, Terri decided. "Sure." She set her coffee cup in the sink. "I'll get my purse."

After stopping by the bank and taking care of Michael's business, they drove north to Singer Island to get breakfast. It was going to be another bright hot Florida day. As they crossed the causeway to the island, Terri could see fluffy white clouds piled up on the horizon like swirls of whipped cream. Dazzling white against the blue of the sky and ocean. A glimpse of paradise that she seldom had time to admire anymore.

The restaurant was one they'd gone to many times during their marriage. In happier days. Built to resemble a beachcombers' hideaway, overlooking a marina filled with boats, Harley's Place looked just the same. Their marriage, however, was completely different. Had it only been two years? Terri didn't want to remember.

She dropped Michael off and parked the car. As she came through the door, the woman who ran Harley's waved.

"Hello. We haven't seen you two in a long time. Where's your little boy?"

Terri gave her pat, obvious answer. "He's not with us today."

"Too bad." The woman came forward with a menu and led her out to the veranda where Michael had already been seated. "He must be nearly grown by now," she added with a knowing, parental smile.

Terri swallowed. "Yeah, he's—" she sat down and was forced to look at Michael "—fine."

"Well, can I get you some coffee?"

"Yes, please," Michael said, never taking his gaze from Terri's face. As the woman walked away, he reached over and covered Terri's hand with his. She tugged her hand away, unable to safely accept his comfort. She'd learned to face the world's questions on her own without bursting into tears. She'd learned to lie gracefully rather than shock people with the truth.

Terri picked up the menu in front of her and studied it.

They ordered breakfast and watched the charter boats leave right on time at ten o'clock. They talked about the weather, about the sailboats anchored out in the inlet.

"How's your mother?" Michael asked. "Have you told her I'm back in West Palm?"

Terri remembered the long silence that had ensued after she'd told her mother about Michael. "I spoke to her the night before last, while you were sleeping. She's fine."

"I'm sure she hates my guts."

"No, she doesn't," Terri answered truthfully. Her mother had been worried about her daughter, and how Michael's accident had affected her. "Now, my sister is a different story. If you want to use a sailor's term, she'd probably have you keelhauled and smile during the process."

Michael smiled. "I don't think she ever liked me in the first place."

"That's not true. It's precisely because she did like you that she's so angry now."

"The old love-hate relationship."

"Exactly. Believe me, it's dangerous stuff. If you hadn't been so hurt when they brought you in, I might have asked them to do a few extra, painful medical tests on you myself."

Michael held one hand up in surrender. "Hey, I know better than to tick off a nurse."

A loud noise distracted Terri from a comeback. A group of disgruntled fishermen on one of the boats were arguing because the boat wouldn't start. The tirade was entertainment for a few moments, then the waitress came to pick up their breakfast plates and pour more coffee. Finally, Terri asked the question she'd wanted to ask the first time she'd seen him.

"Where did you go, Michael?"

"What?"

"Where have you been for the last year?"

Michael sat back in his chair and crossed an ankle over one knee. He looked out at the water, past the dock and the boats. "I just ran with the current for a while, without a destination. I couldn't go back to the Keys. That's where Josh..." He sighed. "Anyway, I ended up bumping around the islands. The Bahamas, Bimini, Andros, there are hundreds of little inlets and any number of harbors." He raised his coffee cup and took a sip. "I just ran, then drifted from place to place."

"Were you alone?"

Michael put down the cup and swiveled to meet her question eye to eye. "Not always. But there were no other women, if that's what you mean."

"That's what I mean," Terri said. She couldn't believe she'd asked, but her heart had wanted to know.

"While we're on the subject—" he reached for her left hand "—when did you take off your wedding ring?"

She pulled her hand out of his grip again. "When I got tired of explaining where my husband was," she answered. "I had a son who was dead and a husband who had disappeared. What was I supposed to say to people who asked?" She tossed the ball in his court. "I see you're still wearing yours."

"I'm still married," Michael said sounding irritated.

"You folks need anything else?" the waitress asked.

"No," Michael answered. "Just the check."

The waitress smiled and placed the check near his elbow. "You come back to see us," she said, leaving them again.

Terri looked at her watch. "I really need to get going. I have a few things to do before work. Are you ready?" She started to rise but Michael clamped a hand over her arm. She sat back down.

"I'm sorry. I left to punish myself. I didn't realize I was also punishing you."

Michael. Terri stared into his eyes and felt a deep sadness. Why couldn't they have talked about it honestly before? When they'd had a chance to make things different? When they'd had the love that should have held them together? Even if she wanted to try, things could never be the same between them. "Well, it's too late to change it now." Two people were being seated at the table next to them. Terri definitely didn't want to discuss their past with an audience. "Could we please go now?"

"Sure. Fine." Michael released her arm and reached for his wallet.

THE DRIVE HOME was accomplished in relative silence. Michael tried to start a conversation once or twice, but Terri resisted.

Once they arrived at the house, Terri disappeared into her bedroom. He could hear music playing on the other side of the closed door but he didn't need an interpreter to know he shouldn't disturb her. He felt her continued rejection like a maddening itch he couldn't soothe. Why wouldn't she listen to him? Why was she so determined to shut him out?

He ended up in Josh's room. Michael stood in the center of the carpet and tried to remember how it had looked strewn with toys and discarded clothes. Or how it had sounded with Josh's laughter in the morning and his prayers at night.

It smelled of furniture wax and new paint, not like a kid's room. Not like Josh.

For one instant, Michael felt the rush of old pain and guilt. It stuck in his throat and made his eyes sting. He walked over to the dresser and pulled open a drawer. Empty.

Terri had moved all of Josh's things. She'd packed them away, just as she'd wanted to, needed to . . . on Mother's Day. No, not on Mother's Day . . . maybe the day after. He didn't know when. He'd been gone by then.

Michael pushed open the closet door and found the boxes. He squatted and peeled the tape from the top of the closest one. His wife's neat handwriting was on the lid. Baseball and books. He reached one hand inside and pulled out a baseball glove. Another foray into the box produced a ball signed by one of the Mets. The feel of the leather against his fingers produced a vision of that one bright day at the municipal stadium and Josh's smiling face as the player had handed him the signed ball.

Memories. They brought both comfort and sorrow. A few weeks ago, Michael had chosen death over remembering and it had taught him that people were more important than things. After seeing the angel, and Josh, and reliving the pain and the joy of his life, he couldn't imagine wanting to die in order to escape the past. Josh was safe and happy. And Michael knew he would see him again someday. Michael would always remember his love for his son, but he had chosen to come back. He'd been given a chance to make different choices, to make things right with Terri.

Was this the box she'd been packing over a year ago? On Mother's Day? He slipped his fingers into the glove as far as a father's hand would fit. Were these the things that had made him try to stop her? That had caused him to argue with her? He couldn't remember.

For months before that day, she'd been so silent, tearless; a zombie in his wife's body. And he'd had the vague sense that his life was being dismantled, piece by piece. Packing up Josh's things had been the last straw . . .

"What are you doing?" Michael had asked, not believing his eyes.

Terri had filled the floor of Josh's room with boxes and she was systematically packing away his things. Clothes and toys were divided into piles. She'd even stripped the Batman sheets off the bunk beds.

She met his gaze dry-eyed and determined. "I can't live like this anymore. We're not leaving this room as some kind of shrine to Josh."

"For God's sake, why today? It's Mother's Day."

She looked around the room for something to add to the growing piles at her feet. "That's exactly why I'm doing it today. It's my last act as a mother." She reached for a Little League trophy that Josh had carried around for two days after his team had won.

Suddenly, Michael lost it. He wanted Josh's room to be here, just as it had always been. Some part of Michael needed to hold on to the bits and pieces of his son's short life.

"Don't," he said as his fingers closed around her wrist. It was one of the few times he'd deliberately touched her since the day Josh had died. In reflex, she tried to pull away and the trophy slipped from her hand. It seemed to fall in slow motion before it hit the corner of the open dresser drawer. The brassy young player holding the bat broke off from the plastic base and skittered under the bed.

Michael watched in amazement as Terri's face drained of color and her eyes filled with tears. He hadn't seen her cry since Josh's funeral. Leave it to him to make her cry.

"It's okay... I'm sorry... I—"

She yanked her arm away and slapped him. Hard. The blow echoed in the small room, but Michael was too stunned to notice any pain. He couldn't pull his gaze from her horrified expression. As he watched, she covered her face with shaking hands and seemed to collapse inward. A sound like a scream was held in by her fingers.

He tried to put his arms around her, to hold her up, but she fought him.

"Nooooo!" She twisted in his grip. "Don't!" Her arms were trapped between them, but she still managed to land a few fisted blows to his chest. He didn't care. He deserved every one. He knew she blamed him for Josh's death and he accepted that. If hitting him could make it better for her, he'd take it. He just couldn't stand to see her cry.

After one last feeble blow to his neck, she stopped swinging. Her fingers dug into his shirt, and he felt the material rip away from the top button. But he held on.

With great gulping sobs, she clung to him like someone who was drowning. And he didn't know what to do.

"I'm sorry," he whispered, but he doubted if she heard him. God had to know he was sorry. If he hadn't been so stupid, if he'd said no to Josh like a responsible father instead of indulging in his own wish to be his son's best buddy, his son would be alive. And his wife wouldn't hate him enough to look him in the eye before she hit him.

Nothing he could do would stop her tears. A dam had burst and he knew he was the cause. He'd called her doctor, he'd called her sister. And then, when someone was there to look after her, he'd left without saying goodbye. He could hardly stand to look at himself in the mirror. He left because he didn't want Terri to have to look at him, and remember.

The memory of that day was one of the things he'd wanted to die to escape. But he was alive and the memory remained, because he had to make it right.

"What are you doing?"

Michael came back to the present with a jolt.

Terri stood in the open doorway with a guarded look on her face.

"I'm, uh . . ."

Terri watched Michael search for excuses and knew she'd had enough trauma for one day. After suffering through breakfast, trying to hold on to her composure—

And now, finding Michael in Josh's room, digging around in the past, stopped her cold. Every nerve ending in her body screamed for her to turn around and walk away. She didn't want to fight and she didn't want to remember what had happened between them in that room, on their last day together.

Something had broken inside her that day. She'd lost control completely and it hurt that Michael hadn't been able to handle it. She'd needed to cry in her husband's arms, to finally weep for Josh. But Michael had pushed her away. He'd put her to bed and called a doctor as if she were some neurotic stranger he didn't want to touch...or hold. Or help.

The pain of that desertion, the breaking of the trust that he would be there for her, had stayed sharp. Sometimes, when the memory of that day caught up with her, she wished she'd hit him harder.

"Nothing really," he said, looking guilty as he shoved a baseball glove back into the box he'd untaped. He straightened from his squatted position. "I was just wandering around the house and I ended up in here."

Terri stared at him for a few long seconds. The evening before, he'd told her that a short time ago he'd wanted to die. But as she studied his familiar features, she could see a peace in him that hadn't been there before. As if he'd found the answer to his grief and the pain of going on.

Why had he been able to come home and find peace when her hope for a new life and her hard-won acceptance seemed to be unraveling before her eyes?

"Why did you leave me, Michael? Was it because I couldn't save Josh?" The words were out of her mouth before she had time to regret them. The peaceful look on Michael's face disappeared.

"No. I never—"

"Couldn't you see that I needed you, of all people, to forgive me."

"Tam . . . I did forgive you. I knew it wasn't your fault."

Terri could feel a sense of hopelessness building inside her again. And desperation. Just being in Josh's room with Michael called back the memories of darkness and confusion. The longing for his love, his comfort. She couldn't take the chance of loving him again. She'd been hurt enough. Why had she let him back into her life? Into her house? She fought against the threat of tears and made a decision.

"If you'd stayed, maybe I would believe that."

"Terri—"

"It took me a long time to get over feeling responsible for Josh's death. It would have helped if you'd stuck around." She didn't give him time to reply. "How are you feeling?" she asked.

He looked jarred by the change of subject. "What?"

"I want to know how you're feeling—physically."

"Better," he answered, obviously puzzled. He took a step toward her and added, "I have a doctor's appointment on Thursday. But what does that have to do with—"

"Good." She stopped him. She took a deep breath and said what she had to say in order to save her sanity, her heart. "Then you can arrange for another place to live. I'm calling the judge to reschedule our court date. It's time for both of us to go on with our lives."

8

"THE TWELFTH? Are you sure that's the only day we can do this?"

The judge's secretary paused. Terri could hear her flipping through pages of an appointment book.

"Yes. That's it. I can give you a different time, but not a different day. The judge is tied up in court, then he's attending a legal conference and won't be back until the first week of next month."

That would mean four more weeks until she and Michael were officially divorced. Too long. She had to get this over with. Having Michael in the same town, in the same house, was too confusing . . . too tempting. And too painful. Even though their love hadn't survived, the memories were there, and the physical attraction between them remained. The idea of reliving any part of the past scared her more than if she'd been the one to face an angel.

The evening before, Terri's emotions had been teetering on the verge of breakdown, and this morning her anger had been revived, but her logic had settled on one fact. If Michael could make it to the hospital on his own, he could keep an appointment with the judge.

But still . . . the twelfth . . .

"All right. Make it on the twelfth, then. We'll be there. Thank you." Terri hung up the phone feeling sick to her stomach. Michael had every right to be furious. She had to remind herself that she didn't owe him anything—not after suffering through the past year alone. If she didn't concentrate on the agony she'd gone through, he might be able to change her mind, make her love him again. And that frightened her more than his anger.

She'd left the divorce agreement on the kitchen counter, then waited until she got to the hospital to call the judge's office so that Michael couldn't interrupt or overhear. Now she had a new problem. Could she do it? Could she sign final judgment papers on Josh's birthday? End her marriage on the anniversary of one of its most joyous moments? And how in the world was she going to tell Michael?

"ARE YOU TRYING to punish me? Is that it?" Michael needed to sit down, but he was too stunned and angry. He held the phone in a death grip. "You made the appointment with the judge at 3:00 p.m. on the twelfth?" he asked, making an effort to keep his voice calm. *"The twelfth of September?"* Josh's birthday. Didn't she think he would remember? Didn't she think—

A new idea filtered through his shock. He'd left her on Mother's Day and now she intended to divorce him on Josh's birthday. Payback. That's why she'd called. She hadn't even had the courage to say it to him in person. "What's the matter, didn't you want to be here to see the look on my face when you told me?"

"Stop it. You're wrong. I tried to make it on any other—"

"Sure." He couldn't keep the sarcasm out of his voice. She didn't believe anything he'd told her about Josh, about the angel. Anger had overtaken shock. *Josh's birthday.* "We'll talk about it tonight when you get home."

There was a long pause. "Our deal was for two days, Michael. Please. I want you to find another place to stay—tonight. If you can't find one, then I will."

Michael had to swallow his anger. He couldn't believe this was his Tam speaking—throwing him out. "Terri . . ."

"I mean it. You don't really need my help. I've done everything I can for you." Her voice wobbled slightly as she drew in a breath, giving Michael a slim slice of hope.

"Don't do this." He could barely get the words out. He needed to find the woman who had been his wife, the woman who'd loved him once. These words, this ultimatum, belonged to a stranger. He tried to feel if she was lying to him, hiding something else, but his anger kept getting in the way.

"I have to do this. We . . . I . . . have to go on."

"That sounds like pure psychobabble bull! This is our life we're talking about here. Our marriage."

"Our marriage?" The careful, controlled tone of Terri's words squashed the hope inside Michael. He knew that tone of voice. He'd pushed too hard and she'd made up her mind. "When did you decide that you wanted a marriage? Yesterday? The day before? Certainly not when you walked out on me.

"My optimism about life ended when Josh died. And our marriage ended the day you sailed out of West Palm Beach. Don't blame me for not wanting to put it back together again. I don't know how!"

In the wake of her angry words, the absence of sound echoed over the phone line. He heard her shakily draw another breath as if she might be fighting back tears.

"All I ever wanted was for you to be there for me. But you weren't," she said. "I can't be there for you now." The truth of the accusation stung Michael, along with the finality in her words.

"I don't want to see you until 3:00 p.m. on the twelfth." She hung up the phone before he could argue.

Michael slammed down the receiver so hard that a sharp spasm of pain ran up his arm. "Damn." He rubbed a hand over his face and sat down. The sting of Terri's demands flared in his chest like the path of a bullet. How could she be so callous? What had changed her so drastically from the woman who had loved him?

Death and desertion will do it every time, his conscience gleefully announced. The idea that Terri could never love him again had been agonizing enough. Hearing the proof in her words was almost lethal. He'd believed the angel when he'd said there was love yet to save. Saving their marriage, saving her life, he'd thought they went together. But now it seemed as though Michael had lost Terri completely. He leaned his head back on the couch and stared heavenward. His eyes burned in concert with the hot pain in his chest.

I can't sign divorce papers on Josh's birthday, he sighed inwardly. *I need some help here. What am I supposed to do?*

Michael closed his eyes because they were filling with moisture. He'd thought all he had to do was explain everything to Terri. He'd believed that somehow, with the angel's help, he could make things right again. The angel's help . . .

He heard a car door slam somewhere outside, and the happy, carefree song of a bird carried on the breeze. He waited, but no inspiration came. He drew in a slow, deep breath until the aching caused him to release it. Damn. Too physically hurt to pursue Terry and now, ordered out of her life, he felt stumped. How could he keep her safe if they signed divorce papers next week? *On Josh's birthday.*

He concentrated on pulling in another breath, then let it out slowly. That's when he noticed the silence. It was like the world outside had disappeared. And his chest felt warm, glowing. The cutting pain of a few moments before was being transformed into liquid warmth. Michael wondered whether the angel would be close if he opened his eyes. The moment he decided to try it and see, he heard the voice.

Patience. You must have patience. Her suffering is real, but fear fills her words. Don't give up.

The heat in his chest expanded almost to the point of suffering again, but Michael didn't move a muscle. Was it possible? He'd tried everything else. Would patience change her? Make her trust him, love him again?

No matter. He remembered the fierceness in the angel's face. Michael knew he'd brought a tiny spark of that warrior's spirit back with him. Giving up wasn't an option. He'd have patience, and he'd get well. And then, before he signed any divorce papers, he'd have an eye-to-eye, heart-to-heart talk with his wife.

"YOU LOOK a little worse for wear," Marsh, Michael's former partner, said.

"I feel it, too. Take my advice, don't ever play chicken in a sailboat with twenty-foot seas."

Marsh laughed. "So, when do you think you'll be up to coming back to work?"

Michael thought about that for a moment. Work had been the last thing on his mind since the accident . . . since his death. His only thought had been saving Terri and his marriage. Reconnecting with his former life-style seemed pretty low on the priority list. "You seriously want me shuffling around here like a hundred-year-old man?"

"I never joke about business. We've got some interesting cases you could handle without having to go to court. As a matter of fact, I've got a very lucrative corporate-settlement case you could take. Big bucks."

With some surprise, Michael realized the old excitement of taking on an expensive case and client had somehow been replaced with a realization—making "big bucks" had never been his true purpose in life. It had been a diversion. He needed to get on with some real work.

"I'm all right for money right now. Why don't you give me some of your pro-bono work? I need a little time to get on my feet."

"Since when are you willing to work for nothing? Are you sure you didn't get a tad too much sun out there on the boat?"

Michael smiled. If Terri didn't believe he'd changed, he wasn't going to try to convince anyone else. "I probably did. I guess I'm just glad to be alive. I feel like maybe I should give something back."

Marsh stared at him for a moment then changed the subject. "What's happening with you and Terri?"

Michael thought of the angel, of his wife. Of what he had to do. *Be patient.* "We're still negotiating," he said, trying to force a light tone to his voice. He hoped he hadn't spoken a total lie. The legal definition of the truth could be stretched any number of ways. He wasn't interested in the fine points, he wanted to put his marriage back together again. And the angel had given him the chance. He'd get it right this time.

"Are you planning to stay in West Palm?"

"Yes. I'm back to stay." He needed to be close to Terri, to keep an eye on her. To be there when she needed him. "Speaking of staying, I need a place to live. My boat is history."

He experienced a momentary twinge at the thought of the *Destiny* lying somewhere on the ocean floor. In what he now thought of as his "other life," that boat had been so important to him. It had been his therapy, the only thing that had kept him alive for the past year. Then, a few weeks ago, they'd both met their end. At least Michael had gotten a second chance.

"You're welcome to stay at the condo. It's empty now, and I'm sure George wouldn't mind. We bought it as an investment, and because he needed a mooring for his boat." Marsh picked up a pen and scribbled on a piece of notepaper. "Here's the address. It's not hard to find. It's the Waterside, right on the Intracoastal." He smiled. "I don't suppose you'll want to borrow George's boat."

Michael gave him a return smile. "I doubt George would be too impressed by my sailing record. Does he have a good insurance policy?"

FROM A BALCONY on the fifteenth floor, Michael stared out at the lights twinkling from the houses and hotels on Palm Beach. The view was spectacular, but he couldn't help wishing for the comforts of home. Of his and Terri's home. He wondered what she was doing. What she was thinking. Did she miss him at all? He doubted it. She'd been in such an all-fired hurry to get him out of the house, that he'd been assaulted by the obvious. She wanted him out of her life, for good.

He walked back into the living room of the luxurious condominium and picked up the divorce agreement he'd read three times. Legally, it was fair. But fairness wasn't the issue as far as Michael was concerned. He didn't care about dividing the assets, restructuring investments or the question of alimony. He stared at Terri's signature at the bottom of the last page. He wanted his wife.

As a lawyer, there were at least three things he could do to slow this down, to throw a monkey wrench into Terri's headlong rush to be divorced. He could begin by simply refusing to sign the divorce agreement. But he didn't want to start a fight. He wanted to start over.

Out of habit, he glanced at his wrist for the time. Then he remembered that the gold watch he'd worn for years hadn't survived three days in the ocean. He'd have to buy a new one. The elaborate glass and metal clock on the wall over the couch read ten to eleven. In thirty minutes, Terri's shift at the hospital would be over. He might be out of her life for now, but he could still keep an eye on her. He reached for the phone.

"WHAT HAPPENED to you, buddy? In a car wreck or somethin'?"

Michael looked at the back of the cabbie's head then met his gaze in the rearview mirror. He'd asked to be taken to Good Samaritan Hospital. "Yeah. Something like that."

"It's a little late for a doctor's appointment. You want me to pull into Emergency?"

"No," Michael said quickly. He didn't want to have any more words with Terri tonight. He just wanted to make sure she was okay. "Just take me to the west side, near the parking lot."

"You got it."

A short while later, they cruised along the employee parking lot. The lot was well lit and not very sinister, but Michael couldn't take any chances.

"Where is it you want to go?"

"Pull over near that phone booth," Michael answered. Being across the street would be close enough. He knew that Terri always left the hospital by the ER entrance. All he had to do was wait.

"You expecting a phone call?"

Michael looked at the cabbie again. An older man, wearing a tam pushed back on his balding head, the driver's accent heralded the fact that he was a snowbird—probably working part-time. "No. No phone call. I'm waiting for someone." He glanced at the cabbie's license and added, "Earl."

Earl shifted the car into park, then adjusted his hat. "Well, it's your nickel."

A few moments later, Terri walked out of the ER entrance. Michael watched as she made her way to her car. He could almost feel her fatigue. Even from this distance, he could see the slump of her shoulders, the slow pace of her steps. When they were first married, she'd come home from her job as a pediatric nurse in Dr. Perez's office happy and excited about working with kids, about helping them get better. Now, as an ER nurse, she seemed to be worn-out. He wished he knew how to change that. He wished he could march right into the hospital and say, "You don't have to do this anymore." But Terri had set him straight. He couldn't help her do her job. He could, however, make sure she got home safely—with or without her permission.

Lights flashed toward them as she pulled out of the parking lot.

"Is it too corny to say follow that car?" Michael asked.

Earl let the car edge forward as he checked oncoming traffic. "Nah," he answered. "But if you say, once more around the park, you're outta here."

TERRI DROVE HOME in a tired daze. She wasn't sure how many more nights of this emotional roller coaster she could stand. She'd thought that getting Michael out of her life would be the final chapter of her grief. It would be both the symbol and reality of a new beginning. But everything had gotten so confused. How had she ended up feeling like the bad guy? She had enough guilt to outlive over her failure to save her son. She didn't need the added burden of not saving her marriage.

She didn't need to wonder if she still loved Michael.

The house was dark when she pulled into the driveway. Michael had kept his word and found somewhere else to go. It should have made her happy, and someplace inside, she found a tiny sense of relief. But relief paled in the shadow of being alone once more. Of losing Michael again.

Where have you gone this time, Michael? her traitorous mind asked. *Are you okay?*

As she reached the front door, she caught the toe of her shoe on the edge of the walk, stumbled and dropped her keys. With a sigh of exasperation, she bent down to pat the step, searching in the dark for the jingle of metal. In the process, her purse strap slipped off her shoulder and the bag fell to the ground with a thump. The desire to kick the door in a childish fit of anger screamed through her. If she'd had a normal life, a regular marriage, someone would have been there to open the front door.

As if in answer to her frustration, the lights from a car streamed across the front lawn. Terri spied her keys in a clump of grass at the edge of the step. As she bent to retrieve them, she glanced at the passing vehicle. A yellow cab. She felt the ridiculous urge to wave at whomever had happened by for helping her find her keys. A few seconds later, the taxi disappeared, and Terri opened the front door of her empty home.

"PHONE FOR YOU," Sara Jane said the next night as she passed Terri in the corridor.

Terri's heart fluttered uneasily. "For me?" She rarely got phone calls at work and never this late in the evening. Almost eleven, her shift was nearly over. She thought of her mom and sister who lived two states away, and started to worry.

"It's a man," Sara Jane added and raised her eyebrows to emphasize the statement.

"Hello?"

"Tam."

An intimate ripple of pleasure soothed her fear. An automatic recognition. No one called her Tam but Michael. The connection sizzled and cracked, as if he was calling from a public phone. Her worry remained, but changed focus. "Is something wrong?"

"No. I just wanted to check in with you, to make sure you're doing all right. Listen, when was the last time you had your car serviced? Checked the brakes?"

Terri ran a hand through her hair and pushed a few strands behind her ear. The last time he'd talked to her, he'd been angry. Now he was worried about her car. She concentrated on bringing her heartbeat back to normal. "You scared me." She'd managed to relegate their last conversation, about divorce and Josh's birthday, to the I-can't-think-about-that-now section of her mind. Until now.

After the emotional upheaval the day before, she'd gone home and slept nearly twelve hours straight. Lost in painless unconsciousness. When she'd opened her eyes, she'd felt physically strong enough to make it to the end of the week. To her day off, and then the court appearance. Alone or not. *Josh's birthday.* The thought still made her want to cry.

"I'm sorry I scared you," he said. "I was hoping you might have missed me." A slight touch of humor colored the words, but Terri let it pass. Even if she had missed him, she'd never tell him. Not after the last year she'd spent alone.

"Where are you?"

"I'm staying at Marsh's condo, over on Flagler."

"This is a terrible connection. Are they having trouble with the phones?"

Michael wanted to say, *"I'm right outside, I'll see you in a few minutes,"* but he couldn't. He knew she didn't want to see him. He pushed aside that distressing thought. *Patience.* He couldn't think of a rational excuse for the lousy connection, so he accepted Terri's. He glanced through the open cab window toward Earl, his driver for the second night in a row, and lied. "Yeah. The condo phone is out of order. I'm in the lobby." Earl didn't even blink.

"Well, I'm glad to know you're all right. You know—" she hesitated "—I don't hate you, Michael."

Michael ran a hand down his face. "I know that. But I want—"

"When do you see the doctor?"

Michael frowned. Terri had turned into the nurse again. What had he expected? That she'd suddenly changed her mind? She hadn't. And she wasn't going to let him say anything important. Like that he wanted to see her again, touch her again, love her.

"Tomorrow," he answered.

"Good. Well, it's almost time for me to go home, and—"

"I know. I'll let you go."

Terri didn't argue. "Good night."

"Good night."

Michael hung up the phone and slid into the back seat of Earl's cab to wait for Terri.

When she emerged from the entrance twenty minutes later, he and Earl watched her walk to her car. As she pulled out of the parking lot and Earl fell in behind her, the cabdriver finally spoke.

"So what are you? Some kind of guardian angel or something?"

Michael laughed. The sound surprised him. He started to tell Earl that everyone had their own angel and that he'd met his up close and personal, but he didn't want the cabbie to think he had a screw loose. So he did the easy thing—he agreed. "Yeah, something like that."

TERRI LEANED around the corner and stuck her head into Tom Sizemore's office. He was just hanging up the phone.

"I wanted to tell you that I'm feeling better."

He waved her forward. "Come in and sit down. I've got a minute." As Terri lowered herself into the chair in front of his desk, he smiled. "I'm always glad to hear good news."

"It's been four days since I asked Michael to leave," Terri announced. "And he's doing fine, I'm doing fine." Even though she'd wondered about him for every one of those days. But that wasn't new, she'd wondered about him every day for the entire year he'd been absent from her life. The aloneness and the wondering felt more familiar than the upheaval she'd faced with him in her house once again. The havoc he could cause by simply being the man she'd loved before the pain of losing Josh had overtaken them both.

"Is he still talking to you about angels?"

"Not recently," Terri hedged. She hadn't given him the opportunity.

"So, he's going along with the divorce?"

Terri felt like squirming in her seat. "Well, we haven't talked about it since I told him the court date. So I'm taking that as a sign that he'll keep his word."

"What will you do if he doesn't show up?"

"Please, don't rain on my parade. I—"

"He disappeared once before, he could do it again."

Terri shrugged. "I don't know..." Would Michael do that? She hadn't considered the possibility. He was here now and hurt. The boat was gone. He'd called her every night for the last four nights right before her shift ended. Asking her silly questions about her car. How well did she know her neighbors? How was she feeling? Then she remembered he still hadn't signed the divorce agreement.

"Damn, Tom," Terri grumbled. "You're supposed to be glad I'm feeling better, not ruin my day."

"I am glad. And I can see you're stronger. I've just gotten a little overprotective of you." He smiled in a self-conscious sort of way. "Since this isn't a scheduled appointment, I can tell you that." He went serious again. "I don't want to find you on the roof again if he bails out."

IF THIS WASN'T the mother of all days, Terri decided as she paced back to the ER from the cafeteria. She couldn't jump off the roof even if she'd been inclined to. She wouldn't have had the time to get up there. First, Tom had started her worrying about Michael all over again. Then, they'd had a false fire alarm with two patients under emergency treatment. Now, in the middle of a staff meeting, she'd been paged. As she approached the desk, she noticed a man who looked to be in his mid- to late-sixties standing in front of it, waiting. Terri decided he wasn't waiting for her. She didn't know him.

She walked up to Sara Jane. "Did you call me?" Terri tried to keep the exasperation out of her voice. Whatever the message, Sara Jane was only the messenger.

Sara Jane turned to the man standing at the counter. "Is this her?"

The man dragged the cap from his head and looked at Terri, head to toe. "Do you drive a blue '91 Honda?"

Oh no, Terri thought. *He's hit my car in the parking lot.* "Yes," she answered. "Why?"

He glanced toward Sara Jane, then back to her. "Could I talk to you a minute? Privately?"

No point in trying to avoid bad news. "Sure," she said and walked over to the opposite corner of the entrance hall, away from the desk.

He followed. "Listen," he said, sounding unsure. "I don't want to scare you, but—"

"What is this about?" Anyone who said that they didn't want to scare you usually did just that. He looked harmless enough, but—

"Well, I think there's a man stalking you."

"What?"

"I drive a cab. I've been picking up a fare every night at the same time and bringing him to a place across the street. He watches you. He always has me follow you home. Don't you live on Valencia?"

The hair on the back of Terri's neck tingled, and her pulse leaped into overdrive. She took a half step backward, away from him. He looked fatherly, but she'd seen enough psychiatric patients to know that they could act normal under certain circumstances. How had he picked her out? She didn't know what to say.

The man went on as if he didn't notice her growing alarm. "The guy seems nice enough. Tall. Dark hair. Looks like he's been in an accident or a fight."

Terri ran a shaky hand over her forehead as relief flooded through her. "Michael." She met the older man's eyes. "He's my husband . . . my almost ex-husband," she amended. Instead of leaving her again, Michael was following her around.

"Well, I got worried because he never wants you to see him and I thought you ought to know that he's out there. Do you want me to go to the police?"

"No." She offered him a real smile, and her hand. It was nice to know a stranger cared about her. In the last year, several strangers had become her friends, the only friends she'd been able to count on. "What did you say your name was?"

"It's Earl, ma'am," he said, engulfing her hand with his.

"Well, Earl. I really appreciate your concern, but Michael isn't going to hurt me." She hesitated as a solution to the problem occurred to her. "I do think I need to have a little talk with him, however. Where did you say you park?"

9

TODAY WAS the eleventh. Tomorrow would have been Josh's seventh birthday—if he'd lived. As Michael walked along the sidewalk through the lush greenery surrounding the entrance of the condominium, he let his mind drift to other times, other birthdays. Back to memories of cake and ice cream and the excited squeals of Josh and his friends as they tried to break a piñata or played catch with water balloons. The happiness that had been part of the fairy tale of their lives. Before one of those lives had ended.

Michael looked skyward and smiled sadly. "Hope you have a happy birthday, buddy. Help me out with your mom if you can." His happiness faded. He missed his son, but he knew Josh was safe. It was Terri who needed his help now. Instead of celebrating the birth of their child tomorrow, he and his wife were scheduled to be in court to end their marriage.

They were coming down to the wire and Michael still had no firm plan on how to save his marriage, or how to save Terri. He'd been patient. He'd stayed away from her as she'd asked, but time was running out. The nagging sense of urgency had come back.

Michael flexed his injured right arm. At least he felt better physically. He'd worked in the office for half a day and then gone to see his doctor. He wouldn't be entering a triathlon any time soon, but he could raise his right arm halfway without experiencing that breath-stealing pain in his shoulder. And his chest no longer felt as though an elephant were standing on it.

But tomorrow was the twelfth. And he needed to talk to Terri. He would follow her home tonight as he had the past few nights. But this time, he would have Earl stop and Michael would knock on the front door.

In the distance, he saw a yellow cab making a left turn onto Flagler. That would be Earl. He turned back toward the entrance of the building.

Michael momentarily thought of his BMW, still parked in Terri's garage. It didn't seem important. Tomorrow, he'd rent a car, any car. He needed to be mobile. As he opened the door to the cab and slid into the cab seat, he met a familiar gaze in the rearview mirror.

"Earl, this may be our last night together. I think I'm almost ready to drive."

TERRI WAS LATE. Michael checked his new watch one more time.

"What time have you got, Earl?"

"Eleven forty-five."

"Her car is still there. Must be a busy night," Michael said, slumping back against the seat. But there didn't seem to be much activity in the parking lot or at the entrance of the ER. No ambulances or stream of relatives arriving. He wondered again why Terri had chosen to work Emergency. After the pain of Josh's death, why had she volunteered to work on the front line?

Just then, the door of the ER slid open and a person walked out into the night. A man—not Terri. Michael drummed his fingers against the vinyl covering the armrest. Where was she?

A tapping on the opposite side of the car drew his attention from the parking lot. Terri leaned into the open window.

"Could I have a word with you?"

The surprised look on Michael's face was worth the trouble of walking halfway around the hospital, Terri decided. He looked good, almost back to normal. He was wearing a faded, blue-and-yellow-madras plaid shirt and a pair of Dockers. As he opened the door and got out of the cab, Terri's heartbeat flared faster and then slowed to a steady rhythm. Would the sight of him always have that effect on her? It wasn't fair. Not when he could walk away and not even think of her for over a year.

She had to coerce her thoughts back to the subject—Michael's following her. "What are you doing here?"

"I'm . . . uh . . ." He had the grace to look a little sheepish. "I'm keeping an eye on you." He gestured toward the cab. "Earl and me."

Terri leaned down. "Hello, Earl," she said. He returned the greeting. She straightened to face Michael again and crossed her arms. She needed to set him straight one last time about butting into her life. And more important, she needed to know if he'd signed the divorce agreement. But her mind was a blank. Words wouldn't connect.

And then he smiled his pirate smile.

"Why don't you let Earl give us a ride to your car? It's been years since I've talked you into getting into the back seat with me."

She had to struggle not to laugh. And for one singing moment, Terri felt new again. The pain of the past lifted like a fog driven by the wind and she could see the fiery glitter of the sun. Even though she hadn't felt any warmth for so long, the light was there. And so was Michael. The man she'd loved for so long that she'd had to teach herself how not to love him.

He opened the back door of the cab with the finesse of a courtier and waited.

Terri got into the cab. Michael slid in next to her, closer than he needed to be, but not touching. She looked out the window rather than into his hazel eyes, and searched around inside for that well-polished shield of anger—her only defense against this flirting, playful side of her husband.

Earl drove into the parking lot and a short while later they stopped behind Terri's Honda.

There was no use beating around the bush. They couldn't have the conversation they needed to have with an audience.

"Pay Earl and give him a good tip," Terri said as she reached for the door handle. "I'll drop you off on the way home."

THANK GOODNESS the condo wasn't very far from the hospital, Terri thought as she turned out of the hospital parking lot with Michael next to her. Moments later, they were in the turn lane in front of the Waterside. Flanked by Flagler Boulevard on the front side and the edge of the Intracoastal on the other, the building looked modern and exclusive, surrounded by its own marina filled with expensive boats.

Terri pulled up the driveway past the covered entrance, and into a parking place. She shut off the engine before turning to look at him.

Michael stared at his wife, so prim and professional in her white nurse's uniform, and drew in a deep breath. He could smell her, the sweet, clean smell of the brand of perfume she'd worn for years.

He remembered an article in a women's magazine Terri had laughingly shown him once. It listed nurses as number four on the top ten men's sexual fantasies. Angels of mercy. He didn't know about other men, but Michael's mind got stuck on the kind of lacy, sexy underthings Terri used to wear beneath her uniform. As a rebellion against too much professionalism and as a temptation for him.

He wondered what she was wearing close to her sweet-smelling skin tonight.

Michael pulled his gaze away and looked out the windshield toward the boats. He had to get out of the car or he would reach for her. Besides, the doorman or security guard could happen along any minute and interrupt any serious conversation they might manage. "You want to come up?"

"No." The answer came faster than he wanted to think about.

"Let's walk out on the dock, then." He opened the car door and the light came on. Terri didn't move.

"Why have you been following me home from work?"

It seemed like a silly question to Michael. Hadn't he told her that the angel had said to look out for her? "To make sure you got there safely. And because sooner or later, we have to talk."

"You're right. We do need to talk." The finality in her voice caused Michael's stomach to tighten. His well-organized legal mind suddenly went blank. Terri opened her door and slid out of the car.

The night around them was sultry and beautiful, with a breeze that rustled the nearby palms. The slight chop on the water caused the canvas-covered boats secured to the slips to bob and shift. Michael opened the security gate of the deserted dock and they stepped through it onto the wood planking.

Terri stopped, drew in a deep breath and pushed a hand through her hair. She'd thought she would be safer outside than alone with Michael in the condo. But she'd been wrong. The memories of the many times she and Michael had gone for an evening cruise along the Intracoastal came back in a rush, threatening her resolve. Warm breezes and starry skies . . . and Michael in the dark. Suddenly, she wished she'd insisted on staying in the parking lot.

He touched her arm to guide her forward. "George's boat is down on the end. We can sit and talk there."

Terri's feet moved, but her heart resisted. She didn't want to sit on a boat on a beautiful evening, and discuss divorce with Michael. But that's just what she would have to do.

George's boat was called the *Dream Catcher*, and as Michael extended a hand to help her step off the dock to the deck, Terri still battled the urge to turn and run. Michael simply stood and waited.

The boat shifted as she stepped down. He released her hand and busied himself with the snaps on the tarp covering the padded benchlike seat running down the center of the boat.

"Have a seat," he said.

Instead, Terri walked to the other end of the boat. The lights from Palm Beach glittered on the water. The traffic on the Royal Park Bridge was sparse, but the headlights and taillights glowed between the railing, making broken patterns on the water below.

She crossed her arms, resisting the beauty, fighting the slow, familiar pull and rock of the boat beneath her feet, ignoring the moon and the midnight sky spangled with stars. She felt Michael move up behind her and felt afraid. Afraid of herself. She thought she'd learned her lesson about not loving Michael, but caught between him and the darkness, she wasn't so sure.

In defense, she took the offensive. "Have you signed the divorce agreement?"

"No."

She turned to face him, more afraid than ever. "You said you would. You gave your word—"

"I know, and I— Tam, I—"

The warning itch of tears caused Terri to close her eyes for a moment. Before she opened them, Michael stepped forward and drew her into his arms. He held her firmly but she didn't fight. She stood there with her arms still crossed against his chest and struggled with her needs, her fears and her agonizing decisions. She ought to push him away, to scream that he had no right to touch her. But she needed to be held, to be comforted. She was so tired of making decisions, of struggling through each day, of missing her husband.

Michael pushed his face into Terri's hair and breathed in the smell of her, the warmth of her. After wandering for over a year, he felt as if he'd finally found his direction again. He was back where he started, where he belonged. And now he only wanted to find a way to put his life back together. Both their lives. To do that, he had to help relieve Terri's suffering. He had to tell her what he knew. What he'd found out by dying.

"It's after midnight—September twelfth," he said close to her ear. "I want to talk to you about Josh." Terri didn't answer or relax in his embrace. She lowered her forehead to his shoulder and he felt the wetness of a teardrop soak through the material covering his skin.

"I remember the night he was born," he continued. "Although a lot of it was a blur. I remember you were in such pain that I wanted to grab the doctor by the throat and shake him, make him do something. I was afraid I'd lose you." He shifted his position slightly, wishing he could raise his right arm higher, hoping she would loosen up and put her arms around him. She remained still.

"And then Josh came. Angry and squalling like a cat that had been dunked in a bucket of cold water." Terri shuddered against him, and tears came to Michael's eyes. September twelfth would forever be Josh's birthday. He hadn't known then what having a son meant. He'd only been glad it was over, glad both Josh and Terri were fine.

"That night, I didn't know yet how much I would love him," he whispered into his wife's ear. "Or how much I'd love you for giving him to me."

Michael drew in a long slow breath. He couldn't stop now. "And I remember the day he died. He'd wanted that new video game and I'd said no. I told him he wasn't going to sit below and play video games while we were on the boat. He sulked for about an hour and then he saw the wave runners." Even now that he knew Josh was fine, Michael wished he'd hugged him a few more times that last day. "I wish I'd told him I loved him just one more time."

The stiff resistance in Terri's body collapsed and her arms loosened. Then she shifted and clung to him as if she believed she would fly into pieces if he let go. His tender ribs throbbed with the pressure, but he held on.

"My sweet Tam . . ." Michael could barely force words through his tight throat. He blinked and his own tears rolled down his jaw into Terri's hair. "I've wanted to tell you. Josh is fine. I know you don't understand, but trust me, I've seen him and I know. He's loved and—"

"We didn't take any pictures." Terri's voice sounded small and heartbroken. "He'd missed picture day at school because he was getting over the chicken pox. And then I forgot to get film for the camera to take on the trip." Her voice broke with a sob. "I can't remember his face, his smile that day. I can only see him pale and still and . . ."

Terri pulled back from him. Not out of his arms but far enough to connect with his gaze. In the dark, her tear-sparkled eyes were wide and solemn, and he searched them for an answer. Even if she didn't love him, would she trust him about Josh? Would she accept this one gift from him?

She looked younger, frailer. On the edge of her control. The breeze tossed a few strands of her dark hair up and away from her jaw. Water slapped against the pilings of the dock and caused the boat to rock gently. Distant traffic noises receded, and Michael held his breath. But he had one more thing he had to say.

"It wasn't our fault that Josh died. Neither of us could have saved him."

Terri stared at him for an eternity, as if she could find his lost soul in his eyes, before she brought one hand up to brush the wetness on his face with her fingertips.

Michael remained perfectly still, afraid to speak, afraid to listen, unable to change the course of whatever was about to happen.

And then she kissed him.

10

TERRI KNEW she'd finally lost her mind, but it didn't matter. She'd been so empty, guilty. Alone, for so long. Alone in a house with memories of Josh and Michael all around her. She needed her husband. She needed Michael. Just for one night, this last night. Josh's birthday. She kissed her husband's tears, then his lips. When his mouth shifted to accommodate hers, she forgot everything but the taste of him, the warmth, the slow coaxing touch of his lips.

"Love me, Michael. Please." The words were out before she could stop them, and Michael's reaction was instantaneous. Moving one hand up to cradle her face, suddenly he was kissing her. Pushing his fingers into her hair, delving into her mouth with his tongue, striking sparks that were never far from the surface between them. Tears came to Terri's eyes once again but for a different reason. Relief. She knew Michael could make her forget the pain if only for the short time she was in his arms. Michael could make her forget everything but his touch, his body. And she wanted to forget . . . and remember.

When his fingers brushed across her breast and found the first button of her uniform, she groaned into his kiss. *Hurry, Michael.* His hand pushed the uniform top off her shoulder as he trailed kisses along her face then down the sweep of her neck. When he reached the top of her shoulder, one special place that only Michael knew, he nipped the smooth skin with his teeth. Terri's body reacted on its own, shamelessly arching into him. And she was helpless.

Michael silently thanked the darkness, the empty dock and the lateness of the hour. He had the feeling, however, that even if it had been noon on Sunday in the middle of tourist season, he would have still made love to Terri on the boat, on the dock— anywhere. Because she'd asked him. She'd asked him for the one thing he wanted most. The opportunity to remind her how good they were together. How well they fit. How far they could fly.

Even though it hurt. As he bent to taste her neck again, his ribs protested. He drew in a breath and ignored the jab that shot through him. He concentrated on slipping his fingers inside the lacy cup of Terri's bra. He wanted the undergarment off, he wanted to press his mouth to her, but he wouldn't rush it. He'd waited so long, but he could wait a little longer. He wanted to do the things he knew Terri liked.

She had the sexiest mouth. And he knew she liked to be kissed, so he concentrated on making love to her mouth, moving and sucking and teasing her with his tongue.

He felt her hands slide beneath his shirt along his bare belly, and the muscles under her fingers clenched. Waiting seemed an impossibility.

Unhooking the front clasp of her bra, he brushed it aside and smoothed both palms upward to cup her breasts. Terri went completely still for a moment and then he was rewarded with a sharp indrawn breath. Her fingers dug into the skin of his shoulders, but he didn't wince.

"Come over here." He guided her through the dark to the padded seat shadowed by the mast. He sat down, pulled her between his thighs and looked at her. Even in the dim light, he recognized the expression on Terri's face. He'd seen it before and it never failed to arouse him. Without shyness or feigned indifference, the heat in her eyes and the soft angle of her mouth told him that she wanted him. Then the sinuous movement of her body as she swayed toward him and the slow tease of her fingers combing through his hair convinced him that she wanted him right now.

"Tam . . ." Michael's whispered plea faded as his lips found the aching, raised center of her breast.

For Terri, who'd missed Michael's touch for so long, the first contact carried the tingling, humming power of an electric current. She was shocked by her body's response. Her fingers dug into Michael's scalp, pulling him forward without conscious thought. She only knew the sweet tugging warmth of his lips, the moist languid glide of his tongue. And she needed all of it.

When he paused to apply his attention to her other breast, Terri raised her arms and shrugged her shoulders. Her uniform top and loosened bra slid down her arms to land at her feet. Michael's hand rose to work the button of her skirt as she slipped off her shoes. There was none of the awkwardness of new lovers or uncertain agendas. Terri knew this dance and Michael was the perfect partner.

She only pushed him away for a second to wriggle out of her slip and panty hose. Then, wearing her white lace-and-satin panties, nothing else, she helped rid Michael of his shirt.

Then Michael stood, holding her gaze as he finished undressing. As Terri watched him in the shadows, every movement seemed familiar, every pause a subtle tease. He looked exactly the same as the man in her memories, yet something about him seemed different. There was something careful about him. As if this night, this time might be more important than all the rest of their nights together.

The thought made Terri shiver as the warm, salt-laden breeze teased her bare skin. She couldn't think about yesterday or tomorrow. Tonight, she wanted the soaring forgetfulness that Michael could give her, and she raised her hands to touch him, to bring him closer. Tomorrow would come soon enough.

He held her away for a moment as he pulled the thick cushions from the bench seat and dropped them onto the deck. Then Terri sank to her knees and stretched out. As he reclined next to her, she pushed her fingers through the hair on his chest, and could feel the pounding of his heart against her palm. His skin was so warm and taut.

She didn't want words. She wanted Michael.

He tugged her panties off and tossed them aside then shifted one heavy thigh over her legs as he pulled her beneath him. Pressed together, head to feet, nearly as close as two people could get, Terri let herself enjoy the weight, the heat of him. His mouth lowered to find hers and she met him.

But then he froze.

"Ah . . . God . . . Tam, I can't—" He rolled onto his back away from her and held his right arm close to his chest.

As Michael struggled against the pain in his shoulder, he felt like crying again, but for a much different reason. If anyone had asked him ten minutes ago whether *anything*, including the police, a divorce or even an angel could keep him from making love to his wife, he would have shouted no with complete conviction. At this moment, he wanted Terri more than he could tell her. He needed to show her how much and for how long, and he'd intended to do just that. Until the reminder of his injured shoulder had stopped him. He panted and waited to catch enough air to speak.

"What's wrong?" Terri bent over him, her hair a curtain of darkness that hid her expression. He could feel the heated softness of her skin along his side and the tenseness in her muscles.

Michael raised his left arm and pushed a handful of dark strands behind her ear. "I can't, Tam. My shoulder— I thought—" His voice sounded as miserable as he felt. "I want you so much, but I—"

"Hush." She kissed the palm of his hand and pressed it to her cheek. Then she levered herself to a sitting position between his thighs. "Move over."

Michael did as instructed. When he was in the center of the thick cushion, Terri rose to her hands and knees and moved upward until they were face-to-face. "Better now?"

Flat on his back, Michael's pain had eased. "Yes," he answered as he raised one hand to lightly trace her breast. "I'm sorry."

"Let me—" she kissed his mouth, his jaw, his ear "—love you." Michael couldn't answer because Terri was traversing his neck then his chest with her open mouth and tongue, but he decided that if he'd died a few weeks before, he'd finally made it to heaven.

When she nipped the sensitive skin on his belly, his muscles jumped and he had to grit his teeth to remain still. When the cool strands of her hair brushed across the hot straining length of his sex, he groaned. Somewhere in his mind, he remembered that he'd intended for this to be different. That he'd intended to make love to Terri in all the ways he knew she loved. But her warm, moist breath tickled him and her tongue teased him and all he could do was hold on to her and help. And then her sexy mouth . . .

He pushed his fingers into her hair as a tremor ran through him. Torn between needing to end the exquisite torture and wanting to die of it, he left the decision to Tam. And she didn't disappoint him. Just as he thought he couldn't take one more second, one more stroke, she released him, climbing upward to find his mouth with hers once again.

As he answered her kiss, Michael pulled Terri downward and dragged her knees to straddle his hips, which put them in intimate contact. Michael pressed upward and she moaned against his mouth. With the next thrust upward, he slid inside her.

Terri pulled away from his kiss and arched her back. With her weight balanced on his hips, she began to move. It felt so damned good, Michael wanted to close his eyes and just feel. But he also wanted to watch Terri, to see her pleasure, to know that he could give her as much satisfaction as she was giving him. She was still his wife, and when she threw her head back and rocked against him, he wanted to shout, "See what we have together? How good it can be?"

But his own climax was building, and as Terri's body moved through its sensual dance, his fingers dug into her hips, pulling her closer, harder, until he couldn't think at all.

"*Tam.*"

With the rhythm of longtime lovers, they reached the edge together, then willingly leaped over. Michael opened his arms as Terri collapsed forward, but she didn't fall against him. She shifted to lie along his left side. He kissed her cheek, her chin, her mouth. Words rose inside him and he wanted to tell her that he loved her, that he would always love her, but he waited, afraid of too much too soon. She was in his arms, naked and loving. He'd have to be content with that for now.

And he was content. There could be no other way to describe the feeling of completeness inside him. He silently thanked the angel. He had his life back and Terri in his arms. The only one missing was Josh.

And today was Josh's birthday.

Terri rested against Michael's chest, unable to move or think. He'd given her exactly what she'd needed—relief, release, forgetfulness. Now she wanted to bask in the afterglow. His left hand absently traced a path back and forth along her upper arm and the contact brought goose bumps. She shivered slightly.

"Are you cold?" His arm tightened around her.

"No." She rubbed her cheek against his chest and breathed in the familiar smell of his skin. She wasn't cold and she didn't want to talk. She gazed upward toward the stars and the moon. It was such a beautiful night. Lying here in Michael's arms, she could almost believe in living again, in loving. Fear seemed a distant phantom.

Then light flashed across the mast of the boat. Terri blinked, not alarmed, just mildly curious. It must have been from a passing car, she decided, although she hadn't noticed it before. She almost laughed out loud. A few minutes ago, when Michael had been inside her, pushing her to her own flash point, a marching band complete with drill team could have paraded down the dock without her noticing. She started to turn and share that thought with Michael, when the light flashed again and she realized what it was.

She edged up into a sitting position to peek over the raised section of the boat. A security guard was making his way along the dock shining a flashlight into the boats.

"What's wrong?" Michael asked.

"We might be caught. Security is checking the dock."

"Get down." Michael pulled her down next to him and reached up to catch the edge of the tarp he'd unsnapped earlier. He pulled, and the heavy material cascaded over them, shutting them in complete darkness.

Terri had the irrational impulse to laugh. She'd been serious for so long that getting caught naked like two hormone-crazed adolescents seemed incredibly funny. She snuggled next to Michael and whispered, "Can we be put in jail for this?"

"Probably. But I'm a lawyer, not a cop. If we get arrested, I'll have to call George to bail us out."

Light flashed along the edge of the tarp and Terri pushed her face against Michael's shoulder to stifle her laughter.

"Shh!" His arms tightened around her as the guard's steps paused, then continued.

After a few moments, Michael pushed the tarp back and Terri peeked over the edge again. The guard had made it back to the gate, on his way off the dock.

"I think we're safe," Terri said. "But we should probably get dressed." She searched and found her discarded panties. She couldn't reach her bra.

"Not yet," Michael said as he pulled her back into his arms.

Terri settled next to him without resistance. She knew that all too soon, she'd have to face reality again. Right now, she wanted the feeling of contentment to last as long as possible, and lying next to Michael seemed like a good way to hang on to it. She brought the hand holding her panties to rest on Michael's stomach. She waited for him to speak, but he seemed content to just lie there and look at the stars.

"Thank you," she said finally.

"For what?"

Terri sighed. "I'm not sure." She turned toward him. "But I feel better."

Michael shifted onto his uninjured side and leaned over her. "You're welcome," he said as he kissed her lightly. He drew back slightly and touched her face. "You're very welcome," he said before meeting her lips again.

"God, you have a great mouth." He ran the tip of his tongue over her lower lip then sucked until she opened and gave him access to her tongue. The kiss was slow and wet, and Terri's body heated once more. He pulled the silky, satin panties out of her hand and trailed them along her skin, over her nipples, down along the flare of her hip, then upward again to tease the soft hair between her thighs.

"*Michael.*"

"I want to make you feel good again." He tugged on her lips with his mouth as he pushed the cool material of the panties along her thigh. "And again."

Terri could hear the words, but the touch of his hand, the wet teasing taste of his lips and the smooth silken glide of the material in his fingers made rational thought a memory. She wanted him to touch her and love her until she couldn't think of anything—not the past, not the future—nothing but this moment.

"I want to put our life back together," he continued as he nudged her knees apart and drew the panties higher along the inside of her thighs. "I want to celebrate our son's birthday." He dropped the panties, and Terri's breath caught as he slid his warm, bare fingers between her thighs, into the warmth and the moistness he'd created. He moved in a slow tantalizing glide, enticing her hips to move with the motion, until every particle of Terri's being was focused on his fingers.

Then he whispered, "Let's make a baby."

Michael felt Terri go rigid in his arms—not in ecstasy, in anger. Less than a second later, she pushed him away and scrambled to her feet. As she fumbled with her panties, he rose from the cushion and reached for her.

"Terri?"

"Don't!" She shrugged her arm out of his grip and pulled on her panties. She didn't waste time on her bra. She snatched her uniform top from the deck and stabbed one arm into it.

"Tam? Tell me what's wrong."

"How dare you?" The question vibrated with outrage. "You think you can just show up after a year and decide you want your life back. M-make love to me—and—" Her fingers couldn't seem to negotiate the buttons. Tears streamed from her eyes and ran down her cheeks. She managed to close two buttons then yanked her skirt upward and fastened it.

"From what I could see, you were a more than willing participant," Michael countered.

She faced him then. The dim, reflected light from the building illuminated her stricken features. "Yes, I wanted to be with you tonight. I wanted to be held and loved. For one night, I wanted to pretend that I had a husband, or a lover. But you—" She scrubbed one damp cheek with her forearm.

"Do you know what marriage is all about, Michael? Till death do us part? Where were you when I needed you? Me—" she tapped the center of her chest "—your *wife*. One night can't change a year of being alone. You can talk about putting our life together, having another child, but you're asking for the past. And I can't give the past back to you—" Her voice broke as her anger seemed to falter. "Our lives can *never* be the same. I—I couldn't save Josh, and I can't bring him back. We can't pretend—"

She stopped midsentence and stared at him. Her words conveyed her fear. "Oh, my God, we didn't use anything. I'm not on the Pill and you—"

Michael started to speak but she shook her head. "Don't." She scooped up her purse, her shoes and panty hose then straightened her back and clutched them to her chest like a life preserver. "It's not your problem. I've taught myself not to need you. The court appointment is at three o'clock. You gave your word. Keep it."

A moment later, Michael was standing in the dark, naked and alone.

11

THE NEXT MORNING, Michael pulled the rental car into the hospital parking lot at a quarter past ten. He'd spent the night on George's boat, watching the sky, hoping for the angel to return. He'd tried everything. He'd asked, cajoled, begged. Then he'd lost patience and promised the heavens anything in exchange for help to save his marriage. But nothing had happened. No heavenly assistance had come to inspire him. No angelic voice spoke the right words to help him convince his wife that he'd changed, that they belonged together.

Maybe he'd gotten it wrong. He tried to remember everything the angel had said to him, but it had run together with his own interpretation. By sunrise, tired and utterly stumped, he'd given up. Terri didn't trust him. He'd have to go to the one person she did trust.

He stopped at the reception desk to ask directions. "Could you tell me where the counseling office is?"

The receptionist barely glanced up. "Room 143. All the way around to your left."

He knocked on the door before pushing it open. A secretary greeted him. Just then, Tom Sizemore appeared at the door of his office. He looked surprised, then concerned.

"Come in, Mr. Weldon." He closed the door of the inner office after them before shaking Michael's hand. "Is everything all right with Terri?" he asked without preamble.

The concern in the other man's voice set off a small alarm in Michael. "She's—" He started to say fine, as a defense against this man's curiosity, but after the events of the evening before, he couldn't be sure it would be the truth. "I haven't spoken with her this morning," he answered instead. "But last night she was all right." She'd been incredible, his mind amended. His memory supplied a lightning-fast replay of his first thrust inside her. His stomach clenched and the aching heat that flashed through him made him want to swear.

Michael reined in his thoughts and took a good long look at Tom Sizemore. His proprietary attitude about Terri made Michael automatically size him up, just in case. Physically, he and Tom were in the same ballpark. Both a little over six feet and solidly built. Michael glanced toward the counselor's left hand and registered the absence of a wedding ring. Had Terri stopped wearing her ring about the time she's started visiting the counselor? He didn't like the idea that this man had spent so much time with his wife. Maybe talking to him was a really bad idea.

"Sorry, I didn't mean to be so abrupt. I'm surprised to see you. I'm sure Terri is doing fine." Tom took a seat behind his desk and indicated for Michael to sit down. "Now, what can I do for you?"

Michael sat and forced his muscles to relax. He was here now and he might as well spit it out. He had nowhere else to turn. For most of his life, he'd listened to his own advice. His success as a lawyer was proof of his ability to reason out a problem. But after the accident, his former reasoning had seemed skewed. The angel had shown him that in his quest to be rational, he'd overlooked some important things. Now, his angel had deserted him.

"I need to talk to you about Terri."

Tom's carefully schooled features didn't give away a thing. "What about her?" he asked.

"Well," Michael began, "you know how she feels, what she wants." As if he were making the most important closing statement he'd ever made in court, he paused to make sure he had the counselor's undivided attention. He wanted to gauge the man's reaction to what he was about to say. "I want you to tell me how to save our marriage."

TERRI ROLLED OVER and looked at the clock. Ten-thirty. She groaned and pulled the pillow over her face. Why had she even bothered to sleep for a few hours. It only made her feel worse. Images from the evening before flooded her mind again and she knew why she'd welcomed the oblivion of sleep.

Michael . . . Josh.

Today was well and truly Josh's birthday. The sun was shining just as it had been the day he was born. The world outside whirled with its own business, not even remembering the tiny new life that had joined them and then left them in so short a time. That was the trouble with life, Terri thought dispiritedly. It went on even when you wanted to shout, Stop!

And today would be different than all the other birthdays that had come and gone. Today, she would go to court and get divorced. Terri pulled the pillow to her and pressed it to her hot face. Somewhere inside, she'd harbored the small hope that if Michael came back, he could help her. But last night had smothered that idea. When he'd looked at her, touched her, he'd only been trying to relive how things used to be. He'd only seen her as Josh's mother, or a new baby's mother. She was his way to recover the past. If she'd been able to save Josh...

No, she needed a future. She needed a future with a man who wanted her despite the past. A man who wouldn't blame her for something that she'd tried her best to do, but failed to accomplish. A man who wouldn't run away and leave her to do or die in the aftermath of her failure.

But she'd wanted Michael last night. She'd needed him more than she'd needed air to breathe. She'd felt smothered for so long. And he'd given her what she wanted, that sweet forgetfulness, that loving, mind-stunning physical attention. And she'd given back. Until he'd said, "Let's make a baby." The shock of those words had taken away her pleasure. How could he say that to her after the last two years? He, of all people, should have known better.

And how could she have been so stupid as to make love with him without protection? The thought of conceiving a child had been so distant. As if losing one meant that you were changed forever and normal rules didn't apply.

She pulled the pillow off her face and sighed, too tired to figure it out. She had to believe that life wouldn't be so cruel as to create another child when their lives were irretrievably broken. She didn't have the energy to worry about the possibility. She needed a rest. And for a short time the night before, Michael's touch had been so sweetly familiar that she'd forgotten he'd become a stranger to her. Since the day Josh had died in her arms.

And today was Josh's birthday.

Terri pushed back the covers and sat up. The sun slanting into the room was too bright. The smell of newly mown grass on the light breeze was too homey. And the last thing she wanted to do was get dressed for her appointment in court.

A beginning and an end. From now on, September the twelfth would be Josh's birthday and...the day she and Michael had ended their marriage.

MICHAEL HAD FINALLY run out of words. He'd told Tom Sizemore everything about trying to reach Terri, about trying to save his marriage. The only details he'd left out were of the intimate kind. The events of the night before. The very personal details of making love to his wife.

"So, what should I do?"

"I think you should do what's best for Terri," Tom said.

"I'm trying to, but she—"

"Are you so certain you know what's best for her?"

Michael stared at the counselor for a long while. The angel had told him—

"Why did you leave and stay away from her for a year?" the man asked.

A tingle of exasperation ran through Michael. He didn't want to talk about himself, he wanted to talk about Terri. "It doesn't matter why. I'm here now and—"

"It matters to Terri." On the next breath, he said, "Tell me about your angels."

"There's only one," Michael snapped, unable to keep his temper under wraps. He'd obviously come to the wrong place for advice. "So now you think I'm crazy, too?"

"Crazy isn't a term I use," Tom said noncommittally. "And I would like to hear about it." In a move Michael decided must have been taught in therapist school, Tom paused and looked at his watch. "I've got twenty minutes before my next appointment."

"What does this have to do with Terri and our marriage?" Michael asked.

"I don't know. Why don't you tell me?"

Michael wondered if the counselor's calm even tone of voice and his penchant for answering a question with a question had ever caused one of his patients to reach across his desk and punch him in the nose. As a lawyer, he could sense when a case was being built against him. But as a man who would do anything, even trust this man his wife trusted, he figured the truth was all he had left.

"Well," Michael began, "you know I had a boating accident a few weeks ago." He left out the dying part. No sense in stacking the deck too high against himself. "Since the accident—up until about three days ago, I've been talking to an angel."

"And this angel says . . ."

"What does it matter?" Michael suddenly felt like a second-year law student being drilled by a tenured professor. How the hell was he supposed to defend a concept he hadn't known existed until a few weeks ago? The counselor waited with the patience of the utterly sane. "All right. The angel said I had to come back and save my marriage, save Terri." He shrugged. He'd put the truth on the table, let the good counselor make a meal out of it.

"The angel didn't tell you how to accomplish that?"

"No. Other than to have patience, I guess I have to figure out the rest on my own." Without warning, realization overtook Michael. The angel had never mentioned saving the marriage, he'd only said he had to save Terri. He pushed to the edge of his seat. "Look, this isn't what I came here to talk to you about, and I—"

Tom held up one hand to stop him. "You've told me your perception of what is happening to you, but you haven't offered any reason as to why it's happening."

"What do you mean?"

"Well, usually when a person becomes fixated on an occurrence in their lives, they're trying to gain something by that fixation. Granted, you had a close call with death, but the appearance of the angel occurred after that."

"I'm not interested in writing a book or starring in a movie about the experience, if that's what you mean."

"I'm talking about a more personal goal. What's the main thrust of this angel episode? What is it pushing you to do?"

"I told you, to save Terri, to save our marriage—" Even as he repeated it, Michael realized it wasn't true—not the marriage part. He stopped and stared at the counselor. He experienced the sinking feeling that he didn't want to hear the rest of this explanation.

"You've come back to town and found that your wife has filed for divorce. Subconsciously, you want to stop her at any cost. So your mind finds an occurrence that is so otherworldly, it forces you to fight. To use anything to manipulate the situation. To manipulate your wife." Tom leaned back in his chair and crossed his arms. "I don't think you're crazy, Mr. Weldon. I think you're a normal man like the rest of us. And after losing your son, you can't deal with losing your wife."

Michael felt stunned. Was that it? Was it simply his fear and his ego that couldn't let Terri go? He'd assumed that he'd have to save their marriage in order to save Terri, but if that was the case, why hadn't it worked?

"Terri has fought long and hard with her grief and the fact that you left her. She seems to finally be coming to terms with both." The counselor's serious gaze bored into Michael. "Have you convinced her to stay married?"

Michael closed his eyes and rubbed the ache in the back of his neck. "No," he answered.

"Then I suggest you give your own motives a good going-over. If you care about Terri, and she wants to end your marriage, you may have to let her go."

THE DOORBELL RANG. Terri dried her hands on a kitchen towel and headed to the front door. As she crossed the living room, she glanced out the window. A yellow cab was parked in the driveway. Her stomach did an uncomfortable flip-flop.

She wasn't sure she could handle one more scene with Michael. Her mind went blank.

She took a deep breath before opening the front door. Earl stood on the step.

"Hello, ma'am," he said and whipped his hat from his head. He held out a brown, legal-size envelope to her. "He said to bring this to you."

Terri could only nod.

Earl started to turn away, but she suddenly remembered she should tip him. "Wait, I'll get you something."

"No, that's okay." He flipped his cap back on his head. "I wish you the best, ma'am."

Terri stood in the door and watched him walk back to his car. As he backed the taxi out of the driveway, she pried up the metal fasteners on the envelope and pulled out the pages. It was the divorce agreement. She flipped it open to the last page and stared at Michael's distinctive signature next to her own.

She should have been happy. The divorce was what she wanted. But suddenly, it felt as though her world had ended.

12

SHE WAS no longer Michael's wife.

Terri squatted and brushed a few dry blades of grass from the low, marble headstone on her son's grave. No longer a wife or a mother. *Happy birthday, Josh.*

She'd gone home after her court appearance, changed into some comfortable shorts and then driven west, into the afternoon sun, to the cemetery. She wasn't sure why. She couldn't talk to Josh. No matter how many times Terri had visited his grave, she'd never felt him here, even though his body was buried below the well-tended grass. She wished with all her heart she could believe Michael when he said that Josh was with the angels. If she could only *know*...

Terri sat down on the grass next to the grave. She'd managed to get through another painful milestone in her life. She'd divorced Michael, and had no one to tell.

Coming on the heels of a week of confusion, a night of anguish, the court appearance had been brief and businesslike, anticlimactic—a matter of paperwork. And now she had the freedom to make a new life for herself.

Her gaze traced the letters on the gravestone again. A new life without the past, without Josh. How had she lost him so completely? He'd disappeared out of her life like a dream she'd once had. A beautiful, joyous dream that included dirty diapers and preschool, skinned knees and baseball games. And Michael.

She plucked a blade of grass and watched as in the distance some grounds keeper loaded lawn mowers onto a truck. The memory of Michael and Josh together, riding the lawn mower in haphazard patterns across their front yard sneaked up on her. Her respected lawyer, fully-grown husband and her five-year-old son had decided to chase the neighbor's dog with the slow-moving lawn mower. As the dog ran circles around them barking, she'd wondered if the grass would ever look normal again. But hearing Michael's laughter and the excited squeals of her son had made her heart expand until it hurt. She'd never loved Michael more than in that moment.

And she still loved him. No matter how many times she tried to deny it, she knew that she would always love him. In the past, the present and in any new future she might find.

Terri shook off the memory and stared out over the cemetery grounds, past the trees, toward the setting sun. She was determined not to cry. Or to worry. She'd gotten what she wanted—a divorce. Now she was truly alone and needed to make the best of it.

Just then, a slight breeze ruffled her hair and she smelled the sweet scent of flowers. The scent triggered a memory of Josh bringing her a new orchid for her collection. He and his father had chosen a plant with a white bloom that smelled like vanilla. Terri smiled. Josh had called it the ice-cream flower. She looked around to see the source of the smell, but there were only plastic flowers on the graves nearby. Fresh flowers didn't last long in the relentless Florida sun.

The source didn't really matter. With one more deep breath, she drew in the fragrance and, inexplicably, felt better. As if the breeze had brought a memory to lift her spirits and to remind her that she hadn't lost Josh completely. He remained in her heart.

Terri pushed up to her feet and dusted her backside with her hands. The sun blazed low through the trees like a floating golden ball and the sprinklers at the far end of the cemetery sputtered into action. No more questions, or confusion. It was time to go home and begin her new life.

"Hɪ, Emilita. This is Terri W-Weldon." She was so nervous, she tripped over her own name—over Michael's name. "Could I speak to Dr. Perez?"

"Terri! It's so good to hear from you. How long has it been?"

Terri could count how long it had been to the day. The day she'd quit her job. "Too long," she answered. "Is he there?"

"Yes. And of course you can speak to him. Just a moment."

Emilita didn't even bother to push the hold button. Terri could hear her talking to Dr. Perez. She smiled. She could do this. Then she heard a baby start to cry and her heart began to pound. She *had* to do this.

"Terri?" The familiar lilt of the doctor's Spanish accent calmed her. Dr. Perez was one of those people who loved working with children. And she'd loved working in his practice.

"Hello, Dr. Perez."

"How are you doing?"

"I'm doing . . . well." Terri swallowed to ease the dryness in her throat. "I thought I might stop by next week and see you."

"That would be wonderful. If I tell Emilita, she'll probably try to feed you lunch." Dr. Perez sighed dramatically and Terri knew that Emilita had to be standing there listening to the entire conversation. She went along with the game, though.

"Don't tell her. I know she'll go to too much trouble."

"She lives to cook," he added.

"Actually..." Terri gripped the phone tighter. "I wanted to stop by and talk to you about coming back to work a few days a week." Then she hurriedly added, "If you need someone, that is."

"That's wonderful." Terri could hear the smile in his voice. "Of course we need someone. We need you." His tone went serious. "I told you to come back anytime you were ready."

"I think I'm ready now. But I'd like to have a trial run first."

"Well, I'll look forward to seeing you next week then. And I'm going to tell Emilita to pull out all the stops. Make sure to bring your appetite."

Terri felt like crying, not out of sadness, but out of relief. Her nerves had been stretched to the breaking point. But she had to go on. If she couldn't have a marriage with Michael, she had to find another future. She could do this. "Thank you, Doctor. I really appreciate—"

"Nonsense. You're a good nurse. I'm lucky to get you back. Make sure you say goodbye to the hospital because I plan to keep you."

Terri laughed. "Thank you," she said again and hung up the phone.

TWO DAYS. Michael used his big toe to prod the carcass of a dead crab caught in a tangle of seaweed. It was almost dark and the beach on Singer Island had been deserted by most. Later in the evening, if the tides were right, there might be some fishermen trying their luck. But right now, Michael pretty much had the long stretch of sand to himself.

A veteran beachcomber, he carried his shoes with socks stuffed in the toes in one hand, and kept clear of the incoming waves. He'd fallen back into the habit of being alone. The one person he wanted to be with, Terri, didn't want him. His marriage was over. Two days ago, she'd sent the papers to the office without a note or a goodbye. And Michael had finished the brief he'd been working on and walked out. He'd been alone ever since. Now he had to decide what to do.

Michael looked out over the ocean, toward the clouds gathered along the horizon and wondered how he'd screwed things up. How had he gotten the message from the angel wrong? He'd been so sure.

Well, he was only a man, after all. Maybe the angel had simply picked the wrong human for the job. He'd gladly give his life for Terri, but he couldn't make her love him again. The counselor had made perfect sense when he'd said to let her go. So why did doing the right thing hurt so much?

The trackless, inscrutable depths of the Atlantic Ocean began at his feet. A man could spend his life, or his death, traveling from shore to shore. Alone.

To the north, Michael spotted a sail. He squinted to try to make out the type of boat. Too far to tell. Pushing his free hand into his pocket, he continued his barefoot trek along the sand. He remembered how insignificant human problems could be when you were faced with losing someone.

He must have gotten it wrong. Terri didn't need him. The world hadn't ended in court at 3:00 p.m. on Josh's birthday, when the papers were signed. His world had been dealt a severe blow, but here he remained, walking on the beach, alone—with no idea what to do.

He still had his job, although after being faced with a loftier purpose, high-tab legal work held no appeal. A week ago, his sole purpose had been Terri. Now he'd lost the urgency and lost contact with the angel. But he remained a changed man.

Maybe if he'd changed sooner, he could have convinced his wife.

Twilight was fading fast, the ocean and the sky melting into one dark unknown, a few intrepid sailors still out there. Michael dropped his shoes and sank onto the sand. He raised his knees, rested his forehead on his crossed arms and sighed. Maybe he should leave. Just get another boat and disappear. His presence in West Palm would only hurt him and interfere with Terri and—

Michael suddenly realized he could see. Clearly. The sand around his feet glowed with an unnatural light. He raised his head and blinked into the brightness, expecting to see a fisherman with a flashlight. What he saw caused his skin to tingle, as if each individual hair on his body stood on end. Michael was looking into the face of the angel.

ANNA CAUGHT Terri as she came through the door. "Terri? Mrs. Pelton is in room five. Respiratory has already put her on the breathing machine, but she asked for you."

Terri waved in answer and kept walking. As much as she hated to hear that Mrs. Pelton was in the ER again, at least she knew Mrs. P would be getting the care she needed for her asthma. Some of their regular ER patients had nowhere else to go and considered the hospital workers family rather than trained professionals.

It had been another busy night at the hospital, but Terri didn't mind. It kept her focused, eliminated too much time to think. She knew how to do her job. It was the one area of her life she could control. And after calling Dr. Perez, she felt more positive about the future. She'd take her time, learn to work with children again without missing Josh. She pushed open the door to exam room five.

"Hello, Mrs. P," she said loudly in order to be heard over the sound of the breathing machine. She moved to the side of the bed and rested one hand on the older woman's forearm. "How are you doing tonight?"

The woman raised her hand and lifted the breathing mask from her face enough to speak. "I'm doin' okay, I guess." She hesitated, then took a few more breaths from the mask. "It was that darn stillness. You know how the air gets heavy before it rains. I just couldn't catch my breath."

"I know," Terri said and patted the woman's arm. She moved to the end of the bed, pulled the chart from the slot and lifted the glasses suspended by a cord around her neck. "You're going to be fine," she said as she scanned the chart. "You just relax and breathe in the medication."

"I brought you something," Mrs. Pelton said.

Terri dropped the chart back into place and looked at the woman. "You brought *me* something?"

"A gift. It's in the box over there on the table." As Terri turned to look, Mrs. Pelton continued, "You've been so good to me."

A shoe box wrapped with two different kinds of gift paper sat on the table along the wall. As Terri picked it up, she noticed that the lid had holes punched in it and was held on with string and a rubber band.

Mrs. P's eyes were teary when Terri brought the box to her bedside. "J.D., the ambulance driver, said he wasn't supposed to bring it but I made him."

Terri untied the string and pried off the rubber band. She opened the lid and looked into two wide gray eyes. The whole kitten was gray except for the spot of white on the tip of his tail.

"Oh, Mrs. Pelton." She lifted the kitten from the box. "This is so sweet, but I—"

Mrs. Pelton reached up and squeezed Terri's arm. "I know you're alone like me, so I brought you one of my babies."

MICHAEL.

The angel's voice boomed in his ears at a level bordering on pain. If the feeling of urgency had been strong the first time Michael had seen him, now it was terrifying.

The angel raised one glowing palm toward him. Before Michael could speak or ask any questions, he felt his consciousness shift. The angel and the ocean disappeared, and he watched the opening of a scene, as if a movie were playing in his mind.

The first person he saw was Terri, coming out of the hospital at night carrying an odd-looking package, the size of a shoe box. Something about her seemed different. Michael realized he couldn't see her clearly, a grayness tinged the image, like looking at something bright and beautiful through smudged glass. Michael's heart began to pound, hard against his ribs. Something was wrong. Why was everything crystal-clear except the one person he wanted to see?

Then he watched as she got into her car, and some part of him knew she shouldn't do that.

"Don't." He couldn't tell if he'd spoken aloud or not. He only knew he had to stop her. "Terri . . ."

Next, he was seeing through the windshield, as if he were riding in the car. He recognized the streets they passed going south on Dixie Highway and mentally called off their names: Eucalyptus, Loftin, Banyan Boulevard. It was important to remember.

Time condensed. Only seconds later, a red light stopped their progress at Dixie and Okeechobee Boulevard. He stared at the view in front of him. A closed car dealership took up one corner of the intersection and the store on the opposite corner advertised a carpet sale. Nothing out of the ordinary.

Over halfway home, yet panic gripped Michael. He tried to look at Terri, to speak to her, but it was beyond his control. He felt invisible, unable to prevent whatever would take place.

The light turned green and that's when Michael saw it. The car barreling toward them with no headlights.

"No!" His body jerked with the intention of hitting the brakes. Terri's car continued to move forward. Michael closed his eyes, waiting for the impact, but mercifully the vision ended. He was sitting on the sand once more, looking up into the stern features of the angel. The sadness in the angel's gaze brought tears to Michael's eyes.

"Don't let her die," he said, his voice choked. "Please, take me, I—"

You are the only one who can save her.

New determination flowed through Michael. He would save her or die trying. "Tell me how. I'll do anything. Tell me."

You can save her.

The brightness began to fade. Michael jumped to his feet, alarmed. "Please! Tell me how!" But the angel was gone. With his arms outstretched, Michael appealed to the dark sky. "What if I do it wrong?"

13

As the automatic doors of the ER entrance slid shut behind her, Terri gratefully breathed in the fresh night air. It always took some time for her to wind down after a busy night. And the process began at the ER door. She carefully shifted the shoe box to her left arm so she could dig out her car keys. What in the world was she supposed to do with a kitten? Who would take care of it while she had to work?

She couldn't refuse it. Not after Mrs. P had gone to such trouble to bring it to her. Not after realizing that the woman understood about being alone.

Terri stopped for a second as she found her keys. When she looked up, she saw Michael leaning against the wall a few feet from her. His surprise appearance nearly caused her to drop the shoe box and its tiny occupant.

"Michael?" As he pushed away from the wall and walked toward her, Terri's pulse leaped into double time. She swallowed against the flutter in her throat. Would he always affect her that way? Would the sight of him always make her want to touch him, to laugh with him, to love him?

It wasn't fair, her anger snipped. She didn't want to be glad to see him.

Michael stopped a couple of steps from her and shoved his hands into his pockets. He looked a little rumpled, like a young boy who'd been out playing in his good clothes.

"Hi, Tam." His smile seemed forced and Terri started to worry.

"What are you doing here?" she asked, getting to the point. He was out of her life now and she had to make him realize it.

"I, um...I was thinking about you and I thought I would stop by and drive you home."

"Drive me home?" Dumbfounded, Terri stared at him. This was too weird for consideration. "No," she said and started to walk around him.

Michael stepped in front of her. "Come on, Tam. I just want to make sure you get there all right."

Terri shifted her free hand to her hip and faced her ex-husband. "Why wouldn't I get there? I've driven myself home for years without your help." Terri's throat tightened at the irony. If she'd known he'd react this way to her getting a divorce, she might have done it sooner, just to get him to come home. To care about her. But now it was too late. "You're not my husband anymore, Michael."

He blinked, as if the words had physically struck him. But he didn't move out of her way. He straightened his shoulders, pulled his hands out of his pockets and balanced them on his hips. For the first time in her life, Terri saw him as threatening. Whatever his reasons, this was important to him.

"Husband or not, you can hit me, you can call the cops, you can try to run over me with your car, but I'm driving you home tonight."

Terri wanted to step back from him, to put some space between his urgency and her uneasiness, but she had to put a stop to his obsessive behavior right now. "You can't keep doing this. You're a lawyer. You know I can get an injunction to force you out of my life."

In the face of her anger, Michael seemed to change again in front of her eyes. "Good. You do that. Tomorrow. I'll even get one of my partners to help you. But tonight, I want to drive you home." When she didn't answer immediately, he dived for the opening.

"I'll make you a deal," he said, sweetening the proposition with his pirate smile.

Terri had to remind herself to breathe. Michael's strange behavior was making her wonder about her own sanity. Her anger collapsed and sadness took its place. Did he know she still loved him? Is that why he wouldn't leave her alone? She couldn't afford to find out.

"What kind of deal?" she asked, not bothering to hide the suspicious sound in her voice. She watched him put together an answer. As good a lawyer as he was, he seemed to be winging it tonight.

"I'll tell you what," he said finally. "If I guess what's in the box, you let me drive you home."

He looked more nervous than he should have been and Terri had to know why. "If I accept the deal, and I lose, what happens when we get home?"

"I'll leave you at the front door." He held up one hand. "Lawyer's honor. Is it a deal?"

He seemed so determined. Terri stared at him for several seconds, wondering just how he expected this deal to turn out . . . if she lost. It was difficult to imagine that he'd show up and pull this stunt just to play a game with her heart.

If she lost. What were the odds that he could actually guess what was in the box? Not very good. "Okay, one guess," she agreed, going along with his game but feeling relatively sure of the outcome. Maybe after he'd guessed wrong, he would tell her what he really wanted.

Michael smiled again and Terri felt her own mouth curl in answer. How was she going to live the rest of her life without that smile?

In an instant, the smile disappeared. He shifted his gaze and stared at Mrs. P's haphazardly wrapped box as if his life depended on his answer. He took so long that Terri almost took pity on him and let him have a closer look. Almost.

Her fatigue had evaporated at the first sight of him, but she knew she couldn't spend any more time with him. She'd managed to hide her love and legally end their marriage. She couldn't allow him to keep reminding her.

"One guess . . ." Michael slowly pulled his gaze away from the box and met hers. But before he answered, a mewling sound came from the box, then an outright meow. Michael grinned as if he'd just won the lottery. "It's a cat," he said triumphantly.

Terri felt like shaking the box. The kitten hadn't made a sound all evening. Until Michael. "That's not fair," she sputtered. What were the odds? "This is ridiculous, Michael. If you want to know I get home safely, then follow me in your car." She made a move to walk past him.

"Tam." Michael stopped her with a hand on her arm and forced her to look at him. "Let me do this one thing. If you ever loved me . . . please."

If she'd ever loved him . . . She'd never stopped. Terri, caught by the truth and the plea in her now ex–husband's hazel eyes, felt outnumbered. Even the kitten was on his side.

"Tell me why. What's so important?" Michael looked so uncomfortable, she hazarded a guess before he could answer. "Is it the angel thing again?"

"Yes." His fingers tightened on her arm. "Please, Tam. Just this one thing and I promise, after I get you home, I'll get out of your life."

Terri shook her head and sighed. Just what she wanted—Michael out of her life. So why did it hurt to hear the words, to think of saying goodbye one more time? "All right."

Michael loosened his grip on her arm, but he didn't smile. "Thank you. My car is right over there," he said, raising one hand in the direction of the parking lot.

Terri extended her keys to him. "We're taking mine. I don't want to have to come back for it tomorrow."

"Okay," Michael said.

She pushed the package into his hands to avoid staring into his eyes. "Here, you can carry your accomplice. And if you don't leave as soon as we get there, I *will* call the cops."

When they reached the car, Michael carefully positioned the box with the kitten on the floor behind the driver's seat. He waited for Terri to put on her seat belt before he started the car. He reminded her to lock her door. He checked the brakes a few times as they left the parking lot, and he drove under the speed limit.

Terri felt like screaming. The only thing that would keep her sane was conversation.

"So, how have you been?" she asked.

"Fine." Michael kept his eyes on the road.

"Is your shoulder—"

"It's fine," he repeated.

Terri tried another path. "Have you made any decisions about the future? Are you going to stay in West Palm?"

They passed two more intersections before he answered, "I haven't really thought about it."

"You haven't thought about it? What about all your things at the house? When are you—"

"I don't want to discuss it right now," Michael said abruptly. His hands tightened on the steering wheel. "I need to concentrate on driving."

Terri gave up. She trained her eyes on the road ahead, unable to fathom Michael's solemn mood or his sudden interest in driving. It was almost midnight on a Wednesday night. No major traffic problems loomed in front of them. What was he so concerned about?

Michael's hands had begun to sweat. As they passed Banyon Boulevard, he quickly glanced over to make sure Terri's seat belt was properly fastened. *I can do this,* he thought and shifted his gaze back to the road. For a moment, the view in front of him wavered, as if the vision had overlapped the real world.

They were approaching Okeechobee Boulevard. Michael's heart began to pound in slow, resounding beats. He wanted to stop the car and pull Terri into his arms. He wanted to turn right or left, go anywhere except straight ahead. But the intersection rushed toward them like the hand of fate and he knew he had to face whatever it would bring.

The light turned red and Michael stopped. The scene was exactly as he'd envisioned it—a closed car dealership, the carpet store. The main difference was that Michael was able to see more. He turned his head and looked left. There were three cars stopped at the light opposite them. Actually, two cars and a minivan. He glanced at Terri again and calm centered over him. He wasn't invisible. He could talk, he could move, he could stop what-

ever might happen. She wouldn't be hurt tonight.
The angel had brought him here to prevent it.

The light turned green and Michael waited.

"Michael?"

He heard Terri but he couldn't look at her again.
He could see the car coming just as he'd seen it in
the vision. There was one difference, however. The
car was traveling in the wrong lane, not coming at
them. It was headed for the cars on the opposite side
of the intersection.

Michael heard Terri gasp as he laid on the horn
in warning. But nothing helped. The beat-up
Oldsmobile flying down the road with no lights,
kept coming. And seconds later, it broadsided the
minivan in the center of the intersection spinning it
into the car on the far side.

"Oh my God!" Terri exclaimed. She was already
unfastening her seat belt. "Get the first-aid kit out
of the trunk," she ordered as she opened the door.

Michael hit the flashers and shut off the engine.
He could finally breathe. Terri was okay, he'd saved
her. He wanted to take a moment to thank the angel, but Terri was already halfway across the intersection. He had to get the kit and follow her.

Steam from the radiator of the smashed Oldsmobile drifted through the air and water spewed
from underneath. The driver had managed to get

out of the car. He staggered around looking dazed, and amazingly uninjured. A man was lying in the street, still. Michael glanced at the minivan. The side door had been forced open by the impact. That must have been where the man had come from.

Terri stopped next to him. He had a cut on his head that was bleeding profusely. His eyes were open but he appeared to be in shock. Michael set the kit next to Terri. She extracted a package and tore it open, then pressed the gauze pad to his head. "Do you have pain anywhere else?"

"My back. It—" The man shifted and Terri pressed his shoulder.

"Don't move. We'll have some help soon."

By this time, other people had stopped. A man with a cellular phone came over to Michael. "I called 911. They have ambulances on the way," he said. "Anything else I can do?"

Just then, a woman started screaming. "My baby! Somebody help my baby!"

Terri looked up at Michael, and he felt as though time stopped. The woman continued to scream. Terri shifted her attention to the man holding the phone. She motioned for him to squat beside her. "Here, hold this." She put his hand over the pressure bandage and then stood up. "Don't let him move.

"Come with me, Michael." He remembered the last time he'd seen terror in his wife's eyes, and the memory chilled him.

The screaming woman was on the ground at the rear of the van, bending over a child sprawled on the pavement. When she saw them approach, saw the medical kit, she reached up to clutch Terri's bloodied hand. "Help my baby. Help Tommy, he's not breathing. He's not—"

"It's all right," Terri said, but her voice sounded strange, without inflection, like a sleepwalker's. "I'm a nurse." She slowly sank to her knees next to the boy. He was around six or seven years old.

The same age as Josh.

Terri's pain struck Michael like a lightning bolt. It was as if he were seeing through her eyes, through her heart. He saw her hand move to the boy's neck checking for a pulse. Then he felt her withdraw. A curtain on Michael's consciousness lifted, and suddenly he knew what he had to save Terri from. He had to save her from losing another child. He wanted to beg for a time-out. He wanted to fall to his knees and ask for help. But the clock was ticking.

The mother pulled on Terri's arm again, crying. "Please help him. Please." But Terri remained frozen in place, reliving her own worst nightmare. "It's my fault," the woman babbled. "We were late. He got sleepy. I let him lie down without his seat belt on. Please help him."

Terri didn't move.

Michael couldn't stand by and do nothing while someone else's son died in front of Terri. He was a lawyer, not a doctor—but he'd have to do. The angel's words whispered through his mind.

Only you can save her.

He moved to the other side of the boy and frantically tried to remember what he knew about CPR. The little boy's head was scraped from hitting the pavement, he was pale and still. A bluish cast ringed his lips. He wasn't breathing.

Michael couldn't look at Terri, or ask her for help. He didn't want it to seem like an accusation. Gingerly, he opened the boy's mouth to check for obstructions. He didn't want to move him too much. Then he put his hands on the boy's fragile chest and started pushing. One, two, three, four, five . . . Breathe. He closed the boy's nostrils and puffed air into his mouth.

Terri watched Michael like an invisible observer, her limbs locked in place. She could hear a buzzing in her ears. A woman's voice. Her own voice? *Please, save my baby.* Why couldn't she move?

Josh. Josh was . . . I couldn't save him. I can't—
No, not Josh.

She watched Michael's arms flex and push. She watched him breathe into the boy's mouth and thought of the hundreds of times she'd seen CPR applied in classes, in the ER. The day Josh died. The memories seemed to run together in her mind. Then the nurse inside her ticked through a long-remembered checklist and realized Michael was doing it wrong. His hands were too big and he was pushing too low. It wouldn't work for a child.

"You're doing it wrong." She couldn't be sure she'd said it out loud because Michael didn't pause or acknowledge her words. Sounds rushed around her and penetrated the inner paralysis. She found she could move. "You have to compress higher, in the center," she said again and pushed Michael's hands out of the way. She bent over the child and placed the heel of one hand in the center of his chest, where his ribs connected to his breastbone.

Sirens screamed in the distance as the emergency crews approached. Terri worked on the boy with every molecule of her newly returned concentration. She forgot Michael. She even forgot Josh. Instinct took over. "Come on, breathe," she coaxed. "Come on, honey. Stay with us. Talk to him," she ordered his mother.

Choking back her tears, the woman gently touched her son's hair. "Tommy? Mommy is here. Breathe for me. Please—" Her voice broke, but she quickly swallowed and tried again. "Breathe, baby. Come on, you can do it."

One, two, three, four, five... Terri worked without stopping to think. She was on automatic. One, two, three, four, five... She stared at the little boy's closed eyes and willed him to breathe. One. Two. Three. Four. Five.... Breathe.

Her own breath was choppy but she kept going. The little boy's mother began to whimper, losing her battle with shock and fear. Determination made Terri raise her voice. "Come on, Tommy. Breathe!" she ordered.

Tommy suddenly coughed and his muscles went rigid with the effort. Terri stopped pushing. The child drew in another rasping breath and opened his eyes. He looked disoriented and afraid, but definitely alive.

"Tommy!" The boy's mother kissed him and made an obvious effort to sound calm. "You're all right, sweetie. Mommy's here."

"We need to keep him still," Terri said. "Michael, hold his head in place until they can get a collar on him." She turned to signal the EMTs who had just arrived. She recognized one of them. "J.D., over here!"

He'd saved her. Michael watched as Terri helped the EMT prepare the boy to be transported, and couldn't stop grinning. He knew in his heart that he'd finally gotten it right. He wasn't supposed to save Terri's physical life. He was supposed to be here, next to her when she'd needed him, as she tried to save another little boy. To save her heart.

As they wheeled the child toward the ambulance, Terri stopped close to him. She was smiling and crying at the same time.

"You did it," he said as he gently wiped the tears from her cheeks. Without thinking, he leaned down and kissed her on the mouth, then pulled her into his arms. "You did it," he whispered again into her ear.

Her arms tightened around him in a fierce hug. "*We* did it." She pushed back to look at him and another rush of tears rolled down her cheeks. "Thank you for being here."

"I wouldn't have missed it," he said in a teasing way. He loved her more than life, and she was going to be okay. He kissed her one more time just because he felt like it.

"Terri? You riding with us?" J.D. called.

"Yeah," she called back and stepped out of Michael's arms. "I need to get him there, and then it's out of my hands."

"I know," Michael said as he let her go. *Let her go*, the therapist's words came back to him. Michael had done what the angel had asked, and now she could go on without him. Even through the joy and the peace of the moment, he knew he would have to say goodbye.

Terri walked over and pulled herself up into the ambulance next to the little boy. She adjusted the oxygen mask on his face and ran her fingers over the uninjured side of his head.

"It's okay, Tommy. You're going to be fine." She heard J.D. speaking to Tommy's mother as he got her seated in the front of the truck. "Your mom is right up front," she said. "She'll be there at the hospital with you."

Tommy's anxiety seemed to lessen slightly. "My head hurts," he said in a small voice.

"I know, honey. We're taking you to the doctor so he can fix you up," Terri said. She wrapped her fingers around his small hand. "You hold on and squeeze my hand when your head hurts, okay?" His pulse settled into a steady rhythm, fast but steady. Terri felt as though a weight the size of a Lincoln Continental had been lifted from her heart. They wouldn't know the full extent of Tommy's injuries until they got to the hospital, but there was hope. And hope was a precious thing to a mother.

Hope. Terri's longing for a measure of her own hope in the future returned with a vengeance. She raised her eyes from the boy on the stretcher, who's hand rested in hers, and looked out into the night, past the tangle of cars and the knot of bystanders, to Michael. He stood off to one side in the shadows, holding her medical kit, lit by the surreal strobe of the red emergency lights.

His gaze met hers, and Terri felt suspended. It was the oddest thing . . . As she watched, the flashing light around him seemed to change, to brighten. Unspoken words rose inside her heart. *Michael . . . I love you.*

Terri stared harder, and the light grew brighter still, turning from red to white. Her breath caught in her throat as the white light formed the shape of a man a little way above and behind Michael. No, not a man. An angel, just as Michael had described. Bright and beautiful and fearsome. And looking directly at her.

Overwhelmed, Terri remained still as his intense but loving gaze touched every dark and fearful place she'd kept hidden within. Something inside her gave way and relaxed, then opened like a flower bud coaxed by the sun. As if she'd been brushed by heaven and given a second chance. Hope.

No one else seemed to see the apparition. Even Michael appeared unaware. *He's your angel, Michael. Can't you see him?* Tears of joy came to her eyes. Terri wanted to laugh or shout, to do *something*, but she couldn't pull her attention away. She didn't want to miss any of it.

With the next breath, Terri smelled the unmistakable fragrance of flowers. Vanilla. Then, the otherworldly glow shifted and changed, and there, holding the angel's hand, was Josh. *Josh.*

He's with the angels.

Before Terri could move, or call out, or calm her pounding heart, Bob, the second EMT, jumped into the ambulance. A policeman standing at the back of the truck slammed the door, and they were on their way, sirens wailing.

14

MICHAEL DROVE to the hospital in a relieved state of bafflement, although by the time he pulled into the parking lot, reality had begun to intrude. It was really over. He'd done it right. He'd saved Terri from something worse than death—helplessly watching another child die.

Now what?

It was up to her own guardian angel to look out for her. He pulled the box with the kitten out of the back of the car and headed toward the entrance of the ER. He couldn't use the angel's warning as an excuse to intrude in Terri's life anymore. And she'd made it very clear that she didn't want him as her husband. His sense of euphoria was fading fast and with its disappearance came pain.

Damn. His chest hurt and it had nothing to do with his damaged ribs. Since the boating accident, through the attempts to put his life back together, even in the otherworldly light of the angel's glow, his love for Terri had never wavered. Now what was he supposed to do with it?

Sure, he'd gotten to be the hero, but where did that leave his life? And his love? He was facing the final indisputable death of their marriage.

What would he do without Terri?

Your happiness isn't the point here, his conscience reminded him. *Smile when you see her, give her the cat, kiss her goodbye and get the hell out of here before you fall to your knees and beg her to try one more time.*

AN HOUR LATER, Terri found Michael in the waiting room. She stopped in the doorway and watched as he coaxed the kitten to try some milk he'd poured into a clean ashtray.

He'd waited for her. Even though for the last few weeks she been trying to get rid of him. She'd thrown him out of her house, divorced him and even threatened to call the police on him. And he was still here.

A fresh torrent of longing filled her. He had changed so much, yet he was still the only man she'd ever loved—would always love. And she'd seen his angel. How could she *not* trust him?

He stood when he saw her and Terri didn't hesitate. She walked right into his embrace. His arms tightened around her and pulled her close. So close, she had a little trouble breathing. He pushed his face into her hair, and simply held on.

"I just spoke to Tommy's mother," she said. "He's got some bruises and they're going to keep him overnight, but the doctor says he's going to be fine."

"Good. I'm glad." Michael breathed in the smell of Terri, storing up the memories of how she fit in his arms. It was time to say goodbye and get the hell out, but he was having a tough time letting go. He wished with all his being that he could make love to her, hold her next to him skin to skin, breath to breath one last time. But he couldn't. And he needed to tell her something before he left. Now was as good a time as any, while they had the small waiting room to themselves.

He loosened his grip and slid his hands up to bracket her face. Then allowed himself one chaste touch of her lips before he looked into her blue eyes. "I need to talk to you about Josh."

Terri surprised him with a sweet smile. "What about him?"

Michael swallowed. He'd expected her to argue. He'd hoped she'd at least listen to him, even if he couldn't make her believe. The expression on her face nearly made him forget his goal. She gazed up at him with such calm trust, his pulse leaped. It had been so long since she'd looked at him with anything but anger or sadness.

"You're a good nurse, Tam. You proved that to-night and every night you come to work." He paused and carefully pushed a few wayward strands of hair behind her ear. "You were also a good mother." Her smile disappeared, but she was still listening. He wished he had something stronger than words with which to convince her. "I was there. I saw how you loved Josh and took care of him." He managed a slight smile. "Hell, you took care of both of us.

"If you don't believe me about the angel, then believe the doctors," he said, holding her trans-fixed with his gaze. "Everyone thought that Josh was a normal, healthy kid." His hands tightened on her face. "*Everyone.* With no family history and the rarity of his heart problem, no one could have di-agnosed it. Until the failure.

"We loved him, we raised him the best we could and now he's gone. It wasn't your fault."

Terri stared into her husband's eyes and waited for the pain, for the guilt to rise inside. But nothing happened. Michael had put into words what the angel had made her feel in its presence. She couldn't have known about her son's heart. Josh's death *wasn't* her fault.

"Thank you," she said, feeling the inadequacy of those two small words. What she felt inside wasn't small; it was strong enough to base a lifetime on.

Michael smiled a sad smile and ran his thumbs along her jaw. "You're more than welcome. I'm sorry things turned out the way they did between us." He kissed her, a sweet, slow, breathless kiss. "I love you, Tam. I hope you find some happiness." To Terri's utter astonishment, Michael dropped his hands from her. "Goodbye," he said and turned to leave.

They'd finally come to a point where they could talk again, love again. A place to start over. And Michael was leaving? Well, this time she wouldn't let him go.

"Where do you think you're going?" Her words stopped him halfway to the door.

"What?"

Terri walked toward him. "Where are you going?" she asked again.

Michael paused and ran a hand through his hair before looking at her. "I don't know yet. Somewhere, anywhere. Don't worry, I won't butt into your life anymore." He turned his back to her and continued walking.

"I love you," Terri said, telling the absolute truth, without fear, without expectations.

Michael stopped.

Terri kept moving, talking to his back. "I love you for being with me tonight, for telling me about Josh . . ." He slowly pivoted toward her until they were face-to-face, close enough to touch. She brushed her fingers along his jaw and rested her thumb near his mouth. "I've always loved you, even when I was angry at you for leaving. Even when you hurt me."

Michael slid his fingers over hers. "You don't have to say that. But thank you. I know you feel good about saving the boy, and—"

"Didn't you promise me a ride home?" she asked.

The expression on his face caused her to laugh. For once in his life, the best negotiator in his law firm looked speechless.

"Look, Terri, I'm trying to get out of your life like you want me to."

"Let's go home." She smiled into his eyes with all the love and hope she'd found buried inside. "I want to hear about your angel."

Michael still looked stunned. Like a man who'd been wandering in the desert for years and had suddenly stumbled into Club Med. Terri kissed his cheek then bent to retrieve the kitten.

"Come on, you little furball." She grinned at Michael. "What in the world are we going to name this cat?"

ALL THE WAY HOME Michael had to remind himself that he was awake. It was nighttime and the dream he seemed to be having, of Terri saying she loved him, of going home, felt good enough to be real.

Even after he pulled into the driveway and walked up to his own front door, he still felt uncertain. He thought of the adage, "Be careful what you wish for," as he closed the front door behind them. Then he stopped Terri in the middle of the living room, removed the purse from her shoulder, the box with the cat from her hands and kissed her deep and hard. He'd been careful what he wished for and now he wanted it to come true. He wanted to make love to his wife, to show her one more time how much he loved her.

Her mouth opened to him and he felt more than heard a murmur of sound trapped in her throat. He kissed her harder, sucking the sound into his mouth. He dropped one hand down along her hip to cup her rear and pull her closer. He needed to get inside her, to reconnect the past with the present and, hopefully, the future. As Terri fit her body intimately to his, her fingernails skimmed up his back, sending a sharp spasm of pleasure through him.

"Tam," he spoke against her lips. "I need to make love to you." He paused to kiss her again. "Please. I need us to love each other."

Terri seemed to fight her way back to reality. As if she'd already moved past the ability to say yes or no.

"I want—" She pushed away slightly and looked down at the smudges of blood on her uniform. "I'm a mess. I need to get cleaned up first."

With a low laugh, Michael nipped the soft skin of her neck. "How about if I give you a shower?" He pulled her hips closer, teasing her with the hard evidence of his need. He lightly kissed her lips and made a promise that sounded like a threat. "I think I can guarantee taking a shower together will turn out a *lot* better this time."

A quiver ran through Terri. She'd confessed her love and felt released by the truth. Buoyed by a shiny new sense of hope and the simple joy of being alive and being with Michael, she'd wanted to talk. She'd forgotten the rich, familiar taste of him, the dark and reckless, very physical allure of him. Each move he made proved how well he knew her body, sensed her pleasures, played her fantasies.

The idea of being free to enjoy making love with him, without guilt or anger, without having to think, bubbled through her like champagne. Talking could wait.

"We've got all night," he said as one of his hands worked the first button of her uniform top open. He kissed the newly exposed skin as his fingers worked on the second button. "We'll get clean and relaxed . . ." Three buttons were open and Michael's fingers were brushing slow circles along the lace of her bra. "Do you remember the first night we spent on our king-size bed?"

Terri remembered, all right. Just the mention of that night made her stomach flutter with anticipation. In order to christen their new bed properly, Michael had set a goal of five orgasms before dawn. He'd nearly given Terri a heart attack, but he'd delivered. The memory, along with Michael's gentle tugging of her nipple through lace caused a shiver deep inside her belly. She'd always been willing to try anything with Michael, for Michael. She wanted to laugh at the idea that he thought he needed to convince her now. Instead, her fingers dug into his shoulders as he lowered his mouth to her breast.

"Yes," she said and meant it. Yes to anything, yes to everything.

Michael's head came up and he smiled his pirate smile before taking her hand. "Let's get wet," he said and tugged her forward toward the bathroom.

He wouldn't let her help. With more concentration than a kid at Christmastime, he undressed her layer by layer, piece by piece until she stood naked before him. Then he made her watch while he stripped away his own clothes.

In the warm shower, he slowly washed her. His fingers massaged the shampoo through her hair with the seductive rhythm of a geisha. His gentle, soapy hands moved over her skin, cleansing head to toe as if he could wash away the past. When he'd bathed her to his satisfaction, he decided to revisit certain places with his mouth . . . and his tongue. Until Terri couldn't remain still.

They started making love against the wall but slowly slid downward. Finally, at her fevered insistence, he ended up driving into her on the floor of the shower. His body taking hers with hard shuddering thrusts while the water pounded over them.

"I think I'm drowning," Terri sputtered and tried to hide under Michael's arm and shoulder. She could barely breathe after the shattering orgasm she'd just experienced.

"Okay," he replied and sluggishly tried to untangle their body parts so he could get up. He stopped midmovement and, with his head and shoulders blocking the falling water, she looked up at him. His face was flushed and there were red marks on his shoulder from her urgent fingers.

"God, you make me crazy," he breathed as he stared down at her. "And your mouth could start wars." He bent close to kiss her again. "Have I told you lately that I love you?"

"Michael?"

"Shh," he said and pushed himself up until he was on his knees. He kissed her three more times as he helped her to her feet. "Don't say anything. It's not time to talk yet. I want to see you dry and naked in the middle of our bed."

Instead of arguing, Terri reached for a towel.

WITH ALL the windows in the car open, they drove down the deserted streets toward the beach like two sleepy but exhilarated teenagers the morning after prom night. They sped eastward, aiming for the hot, bright glare of the rising sun on the water. When they arrived, Terri got out of the car and stepped into the sand feeling she could finally breathe again.

Michael had made good on his promise. The bathroom floor probably had an inch of water covering it, and there were wet footprints on the carpet up and down the hall. Their king-size bed had been christened properly—again. And Terri couldn't stop smiling.

She pulled off her sandals, while the ocean breeze tugged at her ankle-length skirt. She felt like dancing; a spinning gypsy in the sand. Instead, she drew in a deep breath and slipped her hand into Michael's. As they started walking down the beach, Terri squinted into the brilliance of the rising sun and remembered the angel.

"Tell me about the angel," she said.

Michael didn't hesitate. From beginning to end, he told her about dying, about seeing the angel and Josh, about trying to save their marriage and her life.

"I thought you'd believe me when I told you what had happened. I thought I could make you see what I saw, that Josh was safe and that his death wasn't our fault. But it didn't work. I hadn't realized how much I'd hurt you.

"When I finally figured out how wrong I'd been, it was too late." He took her free hand and pulled her around to face him. "I'm so sorry I left you alone, Tam. Whether you believe it or not, I thought you'd be better off without me. I thought I'd failed both you and Josh and that you'd be happier if you didn't have to see me every day...live with me. When all the time you *needed* me." He looked away. "I'd give twenty years of my life if I could go back and do it over again."

"Don't be so quick to give away the future," Terri said, looking inscrutable.

Michael shook his head, kicked the sand and started walking again. "I wish you could have seen it, Tam. If you'd seen the angel and Josh, you'd know I'm telling you the truth. You'd know—"

"I did see them."

Michael stopped walking.

Terri smiled and touched his face. Haloed by the morning light and filled with that new serenity, she looked like an angel herself. "I saw them last night, at the accident." Tears came to her eyes. "I saw Josh."

He wanted to reach for her but was mesmerized by the look of joy on her face. "He is with the angels, isn't he?"

"Yes, Tam. And I'm here with you." He brought one hand up to brush back her hair. "I love you more than I can ever explain. And I know that my love for you is the reason I'm breathing. Will you marry me?" He held up one hand to stall her answer. "Before you say yes or no, you need to know

I want it all. You *and* a family. I want to try father-hood again."

Terri stood looking at him as though he were the most important person walking the earth. But she didn't speak.

"I know we can't bring back the past. But we can start over. Try again. What do you say?"

The radiance of Terri's smile outshone the morning sun. "We haven't even been divorced for a full week."

"I know—" Michael sighed theatrically "—but the divorce isn't working out."

Getting serious again, Michael lifted Terri's hand and placed her palm flat against his chest, over his heart. "I swear, I'll be here. Till death do us part."

Terri's mouth trembled as she tried to smile. "I'm going to hold you to that." She moved in close and kissed him before slipping her arms around his neck. He could feel her breath near his ear. Then she whispered, "Let's make a baby."

Epilogue

"WHY DO YOU insist on inviting Tom Sizemore to our six-month anniversary party? You know he can't come. He moved to California."

Michael smiled to himself. "I just want him to know that we're doing fine. That I've made an honest woman out of you and our second marriage is working out," he answered, trying to look innocent. He wanted to rub it in that the counselor's psychological bull had nothing to do with love. He also wanted to make sure the counselor knew that Terri was very much and always would be Michael's wife.

He placed a loving hand on his wife's extended stomach and lightly kissed her. "We'll have to send him a birth announcement for little Katie Theresa, too."

Terri laughed. "Dr. Perez says he's going to fire me if I don't hurry up and have this baby. Why are you so sure we're having a girl? I won't even let the doctor tell me."

Michael wasn't sure how he knew, he just did. He hadn't spoken to or seen his angel in over six months, yet some of the effect of those encounters remained. There were times when everything inside him seemed tuned in to Terri, her thoughts, her pleasures, her body. Her love.

Just then, the cat they'd named Destiny jumped into Terri's lap and rubbed against Michael's hand, begging for attention. They'd named the kitten after his boat—bringing something from the past back to life.

"Trust me, this baby is a girl." *And we made her on Josh's birthday.* Their promise of tomorrow. He couldn't explain how he knew, so he used the words that only Terri would believe to convince her. "An angel told me."

**UNLOCK THE DOOR TO GREAT ROMANCE
AT BRIDE'S BAY RESORT**

Join Harlequin's new across-the-lines series, set
in an exclusive hotel on an island off the coast of
South Carolina.

Seven of your favorite authors will bring you exciting stories
about fascinating heroes and heroines discovering love at
Bride's Bay Resort.

Look for these fabulous stories coming to a store near you
beginning in January 1996.

Harlequin American Romance #613 in January
Matchmaking Baby by Cathy Gillen Thacker

Harlequin Presents #1794 in February
Indiscretions by Robyn Donald

Harlequin Intrigue #362 in March
Love and Lies by Dawn Stewardson

Harlequin Romance #3404 in April
Make Believe Engagement by Day Leclaire

Harlequin Temptation #588 in May
Stranger in the Night by Roseanne Williams

Harlequin Superromance #695 in June
Married to a Stranger by Connie Bennett

Harlequin Historicals #324 in July
Dulcie's Gift by Ruth Langan

Visit Bride's Bay Resort each month wherever
Harlequin books are sold.

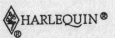

MILLION DOLLAR SWEEPSTAKES

SWP-H296

Harlequin invites you to the
wedding of the century!

This April be prepared to catch the bouquet with
the glamorous debut of

*Weddings by
DeWilde*

For years, DeWildes—the elegant and fashionable
wedding store chain—has helped brides around the
world turn the fantasy of their special day into reality.
But now the store and three generations of family are
torn apart by divorce. As family members face new
challenges and loves, a long-secret mystery begins to
unravel…. Set against an international backdrop of
London, Paris, New York and Sydney, this new series
features the glitzy, fast-paced world of designer wedding
fashions and missing heirlooms!

In April watch for:
SHATTERED VOWS
by Jasmine Cresswell

Look in the back pages of *Weddings by DeWilde* for
details about our fabulous sweepstakes contest to win a
real diamond ring!

Coming this April to your favorite retail outlet.

WBD

HARLEQUIN®

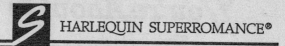

HARLEQUIN SUPERROMANCE®

From the bestselling author of
THE TAGGARTS OF TEXAS!
comes

THE CAMERONS OF COLORADO

Cupid, Colorado...

This is ranch country, cowboy country—a land of high mountains and swift, cold rivers, of deer, elk and bear. The land is important here—family and neighbors are, too. 'Course, you have the chance to really get to know your neighbors in Cupid. Take the Camerons, for instance. The first Cameron came to Cupid more than a hundred years ago, and Camerons have owned and worked the Straight Arrow Ranch—the largest spread in these parts—ever since.

For kids and kisses, tears and laughter, wild horses and wilder men—come to the Straight Arrow Ranch, near Cupid, Colorado. Come meet the Camerons.

THE CAMERONS OF COLORADO
by Ruth Jean Dale

Kids, Critters and Cupid (Superromance#678)
available in February 1996

The Cupid Conspiracy (Temptation #579)
available in March 1996

The Cupid Chronicles (Superromance #687)
available in April 1996

You're About to Become a *Privileged Woman*

Reap the rewards of fabulous free gifts and benefits with proofs-of-purchase from Harlequin and Silhouette books

Pages & Privileges™

It's our way of thanking you for buying our books at your favorite retail stores.

✂

PROOF OF PURCHASE

Offer expires October 31, 1996

HT-PP103

**Harlequin and Silhouette—
the most privileged readers in the world!**

For more information about Harlequin and Silhouette's PAGES & PRIVILEGES program call the Pages & Privileges Benefits Desk: 1-503-794-2499

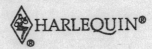

HARLEQUIN®

HT-PP103